■ □ ■ □ ■

BORDER STATE

■ □ ■ □ ■

TÕNU ÕNNEPALU

BORDER STATE

Translated from the Estonian by Madli Puhvel

NORTHWESTERN UNIVERSITY PRESS

EVANSTON, ILLINOIS

Northwestern University Press
www.nupress.northwestern.edu

Printed in the United States of America

10 9 8 7 6 5 4 3 2

ISBN-13: 978-0-8101-1779-2 (CLOTH)
ISBN-10: 0-8101-1779-7 (CLOTH)
ISBN-13: 978-0-8101-1780-8 (PAPER)
ISBN-10: 0-8101-1780-0 (PAPER)

Library of Congress Cataloging-in-Publication Data

Tode, Emil, 1962–
    [Piiririik. English]
    Border state / Tônu Õnnepalu ; translated from the Estonian by
Madli Puhvel.
        p. cm.
    ISBN 0-8101-1779-7 (cloth) — ISBN 0-8101-1780-0 (paper)
    1. Puhvel, Madli. II. Title.
PH666.3.O33 P5513 2000
894'.54533—dc21   99-462232

∞ The paper used in this publication meets the minimum requirements
of the American National Standard for Information Sciences—
Permanence of Paper for Printed Library Materials, ANSI Z39.48-1992.

for Jim

■ □ ■ □ ■

WHAT WAS IT YOU SAID AGAIN? "YOU HAVE A STRANGE LOOK IN your eyes—like a bystander observing the world. You're not French, are you?"

Yes, I think that those were your first words, Angelo, as you emerged from that vacuously bright sunshine, like an image appearing on white photographic paper when it's immersed in developing solution. I have waited in the hellish glow of a darkroom and watched over a shoulder as a special pair of hands performed witchcraft above the murky liquid. The point at which the picture first emerged, that brink of development, fascinated me even more than the shoulder and the hands . . . That, by the way, was so long ago, in another century, in a forgotten country. But they must have been familiar with Daguerre's discovery. I remember the developing tank quite clearly. I'll tell you about that century and country eventually, and about the hands that lost their seductiveness with time. Everything in sequence! There is so much to tell you. That is, to write you, because I promised to write you. I promised to put everything down gradually, from beginning to end, if I can find a beginning and an end.

You are a stranger I may never again meet. You have come from the other side of the world and know nothing of what I am about to tell you. I could lie, could fabricate whatever my heart desired!

I
▾

It was at random you talked to me in that town. No, not quite at random: you chose me because you were sent to question me, and now you have no choice. I never tried telling anyone all this before because people always think they know everything. They prejudge. You won't prejudge, Angelo.

I don't know whether you even exist. Pardon my poor French, by the way. I only dare to write you because I know you too are not French. You're nobody special, no one in particular. That's the only reason I dare turn to you. You in turn must think it is I who appeared from nowhere, from the bottom of the ocean, or the other side of the moon, from Bosnia-Herzegovina, or from an apartment filled with the suffocating stench of an indoor privy, in a small town beside a river in Eastern Europe, from behind a stack of firewood.

Where did I come from, my crime and I, Franz and I ("France?" you said, because I pronounced it badly. No not France, but Franz. By the way, he was half French, half German, from Strasbourg, where we met), my grandmother and I? I saw her in a dream yesterday . . . Yes, I saw my grandmother and a cat called Milvi. Actually, they are both dead, although I'm not sure about Milvi. She disappeared. Maybe she's still prowling the neighborhood, and who can ever be sure about my grandmother!

As you see, I have a hard time finding a beginning. And yet I don't have much to do here except think about this letter. I walk through empty, blank days, briefcase in hand, carrying photocopies of the poems my old men have written (that's my "work"; I'll tell you about it later) and a pocket edition of Madame de Sévigné's letters. I walk through Montsouris Park, where late-flowering double jasmines are still blooming. I stop under the cedar of Lebanon, smell the resin, and dive into the underground world of the Metro. I meet ghosts there as well as people . . .

Actually, I'm constantly thinking about my testimony, because I will have to testify. I weigh the trifling words I have to say about myself as a human being, about my trivial crime in a world . . . If only I knew where to begin, then there would be no problem! Should I start with what I saw a long time ago, in that other century, through the first-floor window of that prefabricated apartment house, the window that Grandmother never allowed to be opened? Or with Amsterdam, that sweet, crime-ridden city? Or with the garbage bin that I threw the newspaper into, the one with Franz's name printed in big fat letters? Should I start with what was, or what is, if what is still is, this vertigo, this blindness, this blinding sunshine!

Yes, sunshine. If I am to start at random, then I'll start with sunshine. I yearned for sunshine. I had a passion for sun, and it was following this passion that brought me to this town where so much of the world's beauty and wealth is gathered, so many gifts of the sun, as well as ugliness, pain, and want, which even gold and jewels cannot hide. Ultimately, to the town where you appeared before me, from out of nowhere, so that I could tell you my story.

My story! Just like the fairy tale told in bygone days beside a cozy fire. A story that also had neither a beginning nor an end but was unhurried and grisly, where one would encounter wolves that killed, snakes that talked, and fairies.

But you did not emerge from the blizzard into a flickering light. Nor are you a gray-bearded old man. On the contrary, you are young and desirable. You are my mirror, my double and opposite. You emerged from the cool Sunday sunshine that engulfed the strollers who had stopped to window-shop, or who stood as though entranced on the terrace of the café; unreal figments of light, summoned by the senseless pealing of the bells of Saint Eustache or Notre Dame or Saint Merri. You emerged from that Sunday void which has followed me since childhood, the flatness of light at noon, which tastes like the wafer of an ice-cream cone. You emerged from the adjacent table where you had sat all along, but I hadn't noticed you because the sun was in my eyes. You emerged suddenly from the corrosive developing solution, still a little hazy, but already exciting me. You put your beer mug on my table, looked me in the eye, and said . . .

So, it was to find sun that I came from "up North," as they say here. I come from a country where the sun is as rare as a diamond, an incredible gold coin that is examined in the light and tested by biting before it's accepted as genuine. In the autumn the sun is stashed with potatoes and rutabagas in cellars. When it's brought out in the spring to be aired in the yard, it has a poisonous odor, like that of white potato sprouts. That odor fills the yard all the way to the woods.

The woods! Beyond the yard there is always a dark, cold woods. Vitamin-starved children go there in May to look for the bitingly sour little yellow leaves of wood sorrel. They stuff themselves with these so that their eyes glow in the shadows of spruce trees, just like eyes of wild animals.

When a person senses death nearing, he gathers his last strength and drags himself into the woods to lie down on the hardened roots of spruce trees, where even lichen doesn't grow. Browned needles cover the ground and keep the iciness of winter alive throughout the summer. Decomposing slowly, they exude a bitter cold smell of death. It's said that out there human souls turn into tiny birds called tomthumbs. They are always chirping away, very faintly, in the spruce trees. But no one has ever seen them. What happens to the physical remains is never mentioned. Does it matter? Animals probably drag the bones away.

Those who value life don't venture into the woods. They hold their souls too dear. They work the rocky earth, tearing their nails to shreds. The soil there is either too loamy, too arid, or too marshy, and by autumn it may reluctantly yield a little rye, some potatoes, and hay. Those will have to last throughout the winter, until the sun's laborious return.

On two sides this country is surrounded by a shallow, rocky sea, which during winters is covered with a tight lid, just like a keg of fermenting sauerkraut. Lighthouses send out warning signals in the fog, but ships still run aground. They succumb to temptations of death, which are very powerful there.

On the third side the border is closed by a great lake from which large, red-bearded fishermen catch tiny, silvery fish as their primary sustenance.

The fourth side, the sunny side (the route by which I escaped), adjoins a series of impoverished, dark countries that helplessly bemoan their stillborn histories.

"The Lord on high, the czar afar," that's what used to be said there. Always was and always will be said, as long as there are speakers, because by the time the Lord's word reached those parts it had become a pitiful mumble, like orphan's tears that flooded the countryside in the autumn so that roads became impassable, muddy quagmires. The czar's orders never brought them anything but misery and conscription.

Of course, Angelo, all this geography is just a dream, a fantasy, because such a country doesn't exist. In reality, all countries have become imaginary deserts of ruins where crowds of nomads roam from one attraction to the other, sweeping over nations, skipping like fleas from continent to continent. Oh well, I probably just invented this country, on the spot, just for fun. Nevertheless, it does exist on maps, just like other countries that, if I may say so, have long ago become pointless and chimerical but still cling to their places on maps. Countries exist only on maps, just like money exists only in bank accounts. People are ready to spill blood for their place on a map. Blood would be like a final seal, proof that everything is more than just an apparition.

And so it is! Everything I have told you is true, the sorrel leaves as well as the death wish, at least just as real as bank accounts and maps, without need to be sealed in blood. It's also true that I come from a town that is as unreal as this city here, only the spookiness of my birth town (what an expression!) is more obvious, not veiled by the sensuous tumult that is present on these avenues at night, by the honeyed light of café terraces, or by the dark, moist glances the phantoms in this town exchange as they drift past, if not through, each other on the boulevards.

The town from which I fled—headlong yet looking back, like so many others who have escaped from there—is a gray cluster of forsaken houses by the edge of a bleak landscape. When it first appears from behind flat fields and willow brush, it can easily be mistaken for the camp of some nomadic tribe, something that will be folded up the next day in order to move on, so that by midday only trampled grass and horse dung remain. Dawn is near. It's time to start moving. The new millennium is approaching. Roll up the tents and get a move on!

As one gets closer, the camp impression of course disappears. Then a stranger would be more likely to notice the potholes in the streets and the occasional gray, half-burned houses. The sea breeze blows bitter, salty sand in one's face, and plump, white seagulls shriek high in the sky. They land only to fight over fish entrails on top of garbage bins and to disperse white strips of paper and plastic over the yard. Those threaten to fly off as well but remain after all, entrapped by the houses.

During daytime people sell Baltic herring from wooden crates on street corners, tiny, cold fish whose wide-open red eyes glare at the March sky. On the next corner one can buy fake American cigarettes, made in Poland, and Chiquita bananas, which are generally considered the symbol of the coming new prosperity.

In winter it turns dark already in the early afternoon, and then people lurch along icy pavements from one rare street-lamp to the next, hardly seeing each other's gray faces. But after seven or eight o'clock the streets rapidly empty of vendors as well as pedestrians, and then only some old hag will startle you as she appears from behind an arcade and with the help of a flashlight offers to sell you roses as red as blood. If you buy, the bouquet in your hand may turn out to be frozen clods of earth. But if you don't buy, then the hag will disappear the next second, and you'll never see her again.

But when it's June, night may never arrive, and then, on streets empty of humans, only trees rustle beneath the sparkling sky. In that town trees grow tall and wild. No one ever trims them. Black-currant bushes thrive in neglected backyards right in the center of town, poisoning the white nights with their sweet scent.

The only carriers of transcendence in this town at night are trams, brightly lit, half-empty cars swaying through the darkness or the gloomy dusk, swinging as they make the curves, splitting the night air with the wail of screeching wheels.

Early this spring, just before I fled, I lived in one of the gray houses with the peeling stucco, in a high-ceilinged postwar apartment where a window looked out on a tram stop. I often watched the late trams from there. They would arrive, open their doors. No one would exit, no one enter. A few figures might be dozing in the blue neon light inside the cars. Then the doors would fold shut and the tram disappear from my sight as if it had disappeared from the face of the earth. Occasionally someone did exit. The person I longed and waited for occasionally exited the tram. And then February passed and I no longer longed for him. But he still came, as if mocking me, and maybe he's still coming, breathing his hot human breath even today on the dirty stone walls of the stairwell. I don't know, because one morning I myself stepped into a tram and rode away, to leave that dying century, to commit my crime under the sun, to meet you, and to give this testimony.

Believe me, Angelo, my movements were calm and precise. My hands didn't shake. I didn't feel in the least that what I was doing was dramatic or momentous. I was observing myself with fascination, even excitement, like a movie or, more accurately, like a dream, because my dreams are often like movies where I simultaneously observe myself and participate in the action. I actually remember it as though it were a movie, and I have no feelings of regret. Possibly just a shadow of regret, tinged with doubt, that it was not a movie, not even a dream.

Sometimes crime reports in newspapers (which I always read with a lot of empathy) say, "At that moment the decision was made which later led to tragic consequences." The decision! It happened the moment I opened Franz's refrigerator to look for the bottle of tonic water, the moment the bulb lit up the inside of the refrigerator to shed a soft glow on that altar of food. The care with which everything had been packaged! The extravagance of tastes! Yogurt with so many varieties of fresh fruits! Pâté de foie gras! Fresh, crisp lettuce! Cooked ham iridescent in wrapped plastic! Bottles that instantly misted over, like the shy but eager glances of virgins.

At that moment I knew exactly what I would do, and I sensed a sharp, powerful twinge of pleasure. That kitchen had always challenged me to defile it, but I had repressed the urge until then. That hallowed place! The walls were spotless, cream-colored off-white. The matte-finished stainless-steel sinks sparkled. There was always hot water from the tap. The microwave timer chimed like tiny altar bells in the hands of choirboys. Dishes were stacked and dried on dishwasher racks every morning, as though food had never soiled them. And finally, the refrigerator with its soft glow, the heart of it all, the storage place for the sacred host. That kitchen with its absolute, clinically clean functionality always gave me this feeling of immense respect mixed with a sense of unearthliness. I admired the porcelain and stainless-steel surfaces as I stroked them. I never detected a single defect, and I felt pleasure in the faint lemony smell of the dishwashing liquid. But at the same time I had this urgent desire to deface it all, to expose the chaos that lay beneath those surfaces, always on the brink of exposure: dirty cracks covering the walls, mud and blood bursting from the pipes, acrid smoke coming from the microwave, shattered shards filling the dishwasher, the decomposed head of a corpse stinking up the refrigerator!

At that moment I heard the sparkling and joyous *Allegro* of one of Mozart's symphonies coming from a compact disc in the living room. The CD player had been turned down, and it seemed that this pure sound, free of any distracting noises, was being exuded by the walls and carpets, just like the softly dispersed light from the lamps. And as I opened the refrigerator door and still sensed the ever-present faint smell of death, all of a sudden I had this crazy, violent wish that the joyous sounds of the *Allegro* would be deafening, that the light would be blinding, and that nothing would ever diminish the orgy of sun and death.

And at that moment I knew I had to do it. With one blow I had to spoil it all, at once, and I knew exactly how I would do it.

But first, my dear Angelo, in terms of both chronology and relevance, perhaps one ought to start with those other crimes, from the beginning, those that keep being repeated like monotonous refrains throughout one's life. Yes, I have to remind myself about what happened in that distant, unreal century before I stepped on the tram and departed. By the way, the day I left was a Good Friday. The previous day's sleet storm had covered the street with a sheet of ice on which a cold April sun was playing gruesome havoc. This made the hammer blows that nailed living flesh to the cross an indisputable fact. At the same time it reaffirmed the finality of everything that had begun: there was no way back.

So now I'd like to describe for you some views that were seen through a more or less forgotten window, to recall some dreams in which an entire little life was depicted totally as well as figuratively.

Who wouldn't want to do just that? Everyone would, because what would be sweeter than finding a victim, cornering him, and then bringing out one's little tale . . . To lay on a counter one's life, one's wishes, dreams, crimes, and complexes; perhaps someone would be interested, for half price, for free! See, this is my story, repeat it just like this, in memory of me: "I . . ."

I'm not actually sure I want to tell this story; perhaps I'd just as soon listen to someone else's. Yes, if there were a voice that would speak, an unbroken voice that would tell me its story, would quiet me, lull me to sleep, relax me. Either a celestial or a temporal voice, the main thing would be that it wouldn't stop, would just keep on talking.

It's to fill the silence that I talk. A silent world frightens me, and then I start talking. I take it upon myself to play the world's role and to fill the silence I cannot stand, which no one can stand. That I am sure of, no matter what they say.

In other words, I will tell my story. But what story? I don't have a story. As far as I can remember, nothing much ever happened to me. My life has always been one and the same. All right, I do remember landscapes, rooms, and people, but my own life has been within them as in an empty room: a few trivial pieces of furniture that could be found anywhere, day and night that alternate there like everywhere else, the differences in light during different seasons, wallpaper that fades with time . . . What color was it again? I can't remember!

Have you been to the Orangerie? There's a painting by Matisse there called *The Boudoir,* a room that has seen lots of sunshine so that everything looks very bleached, faded: only a few rose, yellow, and pale blue lines. I would gladly be one of those in that picture, either one, the one who stands at the window or the other who dozes with a cat in his lap, half slouched in the armchair.

No, of course something does occasionally happen to me, very occasionally: an occasion. For example, when I met you. Then

I start. It's as if I were awakened from a dream. I flinch. I rub my eyes. But it's already fading. Memory can't catch the dream, can't reclaim it. It's already far and in a fog. It's already beckoning from the opposite shore where the sun is making itself a soft bed, where everything faded even before it began.

Landscapes . . . Angelo, I ought to be able to describe at least one of the landscapes that has made me stop, that has enclosed me in its sweet prison and has made me who I am.

My favorite landscape, my ideal place, would be the following: a totally flat grass-covered seashore, empty as far as the eye can see. The grass would be bent close to the ground by an unrelenting wind. The colors would change according to the weather, the season, and the hour. Sometimes it would be dark blue and glistening robustly, at other times reddish yellow and arid, as if about to flare up, but never actually flaming. The skies would be circling in an absentminded carousel. Rain, flapping its resplendent lapels, would pass in a festive procession, letting its pricey coattail drag along in the dust, only to depart nonchalantly over water. At night an idle moon would shine, or if no moon, then stars would chirp in the grass like crickets who have lost their way. Rarely a flock of wild geese would appear out of the early morning mist to alight and gorge themselves before a hurried departure for faraway shores . . .

I haven't seen such a landscape yet, but I would gladly be the grass on that waterside meadow, low grass, stiff from salt, with tiny, light green flowers that would happily yield the golden dust of pollen to a constantly cool wind, letting itself be fertilized by the same wind with love from similar flowers, inheriting a gentle ripeness as a crowning glory. Grass, born from the most basic yearning for sun, ready for submissive death.

But being human and not turning into grass during this lifetime, I would at least like to live on such a flatland and to trample on such stubborn grass according to human laws. In any case, in the end the grass will be the winner, will outlive us as well as our daydreams, and will one day fling its arrogant triumphal song toward the sky.

(My longing to share in the kingdom of plants is actually a yearning to be accepted as a winner, one of the strong ones. I'm ready to betray my miserable race and to sell its warm blood for some sweet, intoxicating nectar!)

There should be at least one building on this seaside meadow, perfectly white and cube shaped, only one room with a window in each direction—north, south, east, and west—so that day and night could move through it freely, without obstruction, without getting caught in corners where old shadows, melancholia, and bitter dust might have gathered. In such a place I would wake with a song every morning, exactly at the point of dawn, and every evening I would fall asleep immediately, because the joys of the day would have exhausted me.

Oh! I can already see your gentle ironic smile! Truly, forgive me, I have already deviated from the truth, first by telling you about landscapes that have never been nor ever will be rather than the ones I'm familiar with. And second, I distorted even these dreams. Because to that dream of cleanliness I should right away add another, actually shout out another, its twin brother, not even its opposite—what opposite? its mate, its skin and parasite—that other lust, the lust for mud and dirt (but even grass sprouts out of dust and decay), an irresistible urge to be soiled and befouled, raped and pawed, to wallow in the warm lap of pleasure and pain, to taste whether your seed, Angelo, may be just as sweet as the grassy nectar!

If there's anything in my life that I remember well, it's the day I went to buy tickets for Amsterdam from the Gare du Nord. Franz and I had agreed that we would meet at a church in Amsterdam, so a few days earlier I went to the Gare du Nord to buy tickets. It was some kind of holiday, the second day of a long weekend. I clearly remember people's alarmed looks. They didn't know what to do with themselves. Everyone was outside jamming the sidewalks to *lécher les vitrines,* as they so aptly say here (according to Robert's dictionary: "to view store windows closely and with great pleasure").

Right, it must have been Ascension; I looked it up on the calendar. In that distant era in the lost country where I once wandered, the village women used to say (they are probably still saying) that even grass does not grow on Ascension. That's how holy the holiday is. That's when the shutters of heaven are open, so those who die on that day will go directly to heaven.

Oh, Angelo, if only I had met you before that cold and foreboding Ascension Eve! Then everything would have gone differently. I would not have gone to the Gare du Nord to buy those tickets, because you would have invited me to an expensive restaurant where the waiters would have been attractive young men who would have poured the wine like novice priests. The Ascension Day sun would have sparkled above the terrace, imbuing all creation with a feeling of ultimate frivolity.

But no, the time for you to appear was not yet ripe. The heavenly shutters were firmly closed as I stood in line at the Gare du Nord ticket counter, waiting to receive my fate, stamped, numbered, and paid for. All that had to be done before getting on was to have the tickets punched.

How strange that I should remember that day so vividly. For example, I remember that the Romanian girl was begging in the Metro again. She has an elongated girlish body, thin as a match, and a long, thick braid. Every day, in the same monotonous voice, she keeps repeating her Christmas verse to essentially the same audience: "Messieurs-dames, I'm a Romanian refugee. I have two little brothers. Neither my father nor my mother has work. They get no welfare. Give a few francs or restaurant vouchers so that my little brothers can eat . . . Thank you in advance . . ." She recites this verse, always in the same accent, making mistakes in the same places. I wonder whether she even understands what she's saying. Then she walks through the car extending her thin arm, jiggling two coins in the palm of her hand. I've never seen her get anything. She is as ugly as girls her age often are, not cute in the least. Why would she arouse anyone's sympathy?

At the next station the Romanian girl changed places with an old man who announced that he was a Yugoslav refugee and played this wistful song on his accordion, utterly mechanically and indifferently. It may have been the only tune he knew. Meanwhile his son went up and down the cars in time to the music, shaking a plastic cup for donations. They didn't get anything either, but they probably collected something during the length of the day.

I no longer give anything. At first I didn't know how to refuse, especially when I was solicited directly on the streets. How could I say I didn't have anything when I had money in my pocket? Now I know. Never look them in the eye but shake your head. Anyway, they don't bother me anymore like they used to. That was terrible. They would spot me from the other end of the street. Those beggars could smell easy prey from afar!

From the newspaper stand at the Gare du Nord I bought a copy of *Libération,* and it was good that I did, because the line behind the window was long and the black man just ahead of me took at least fifteen minutes to buy his ticket. I don't know where he wanted to go. Newspapers are really thick here. They are good for helping time pass. After you've read the paper, the evening is a lot closer.

I remember a big headline on the front page: L'ASCENSION DES CONTRÔLES D'IDENTITÉ. To pass time and out of professional habit, I actually started thinking how I would translate this elegantly cynical headline into that distant peasant vernacular that I'm translating the old men's poetry into. I couldn't do it!

By the way, yesterday I saw what that Ascension Day newspaper had written about: police were body-searching addicts lolling around the Beaubourg, colored people who looked down-and-out, presumptive hoboes, and other suspicious-looking types. I felt a vague elation when I marched past. Oh, if they only knew the kind of fish that was just then slipping through their net! No one is looking for me, by the way. Nothing happened after all. I threw away the newspaper with Franz's obituary, and my documents are in order. True enough, I did go to Amsterdam without a visa. The French police checked passports on the return trip, but they had nothing to say, even though it was an East European passport. They held it at a distance as though it were a monster they'd never seen before, as if it might bite them or spray foul liquid on their uniforms.

So on that Saturday in May I was standing in the ticket line at the Gare du Nord. I had studied the electronic signs above the ticket windows very carefully before getting in line. I have a fear of being in the wrong line, or in the wrong place. I don't feel secure even when I'm in the right place. You can never be sure that your standing there is actually permitted. The sign above the adjacent window indicated that the cashier would close for lunch at one o'clock, and it was already after one, but people were still confidently lining up. Quite an uproar started when the cashier tried to close the window. They would have attacked her had they been able to catch her, but because they couldn't, they almost started attacking each other instead. All demanded their rights!

People here are simply used to feeling that they have rights. I can't help it, but to me this seems very strange. I myself wouldn't mind at all belonging to these righteous ones, to be able to fill my shopping cart at the Auchan supermarket once a week with mountains of bottles of mineral water, heaps of toilet-paper rolls, detergent, pâtés, cheeses, and bran breads, to berate the cashier at the Gare du Nord. But it's probably too late for me to start now. It would be pointless at this juncture. I don't think my rights would last very long, and will even theirs last forever?

On the way home a white woman, about seven months pregnant, maybe even French, was begging in the Metro, and she was given money, because she gave an impression of demanding. Even she had assumed this right!

Another thing I remember from that day is that when I got back to the hotel, or boardinghouse, I bought two tokens and started the wash in the washing machine. I ate what I had bought from the Arab. I ate too much and fell asleep, and when I awoke I actually would rather have been dead.

But I couldn't be dead, because the ticket for Amsterdam was in my pocket. Consequently, I had to go to Amsterdam before dying, so that all crimes, everything that had been pre-destined, would happen after all.

I even remember the dream that I had that day. We were burying a boy who was supposed to smile in the coffin. They pulled up the corners of his mouth and then hurriedly pulled a white sheet over him, but when they peeked under one end, he giggled hideously several times, and in the end he got tired and ran off from the coffin.

A lot of time has passed in the interim. Doesn't this sentence sound absurd? Passed where? And how much is a lot?

It was yesterday. It was just now. It was five years ago. I don't remember. Anyway, I haven't written you in the interim. I just read what I had written and it seemed childish but factual. That's how it went. It always went like that. Just as I have written, without believing it myself. I've written it as if in a dream, in a delirium, and somehow, later, it has all happened. Or have I made it happen? Or have others made it happen?

I write you letters that I never mail. The letters that I do send you are actually shortened translations of those others, inadequate and bad retellings. I don't really know what I've written you. As soon as I have mailed your letters, I totally forget them. Sometimes I study the sheets that were under the papers I wrote on. The traces made by the ballpoint pen and by my hand are barely visible. I recognize words that to my knowledge my hand has never written. But nothing remains of the letters I actually write every day, the ones I feverishly inscribe on the memory track of this machine. Not even slight traces of those remain. They are so light! They only exist as a kind of numerical probability, which I don't understand at all. They can fade in a moment, or I can erase them.

Just as what happened with Franz. The phone rang in his apartment, but he didn't pick up the receiver. I stood there, but I didn't take the receiver either, because it could only have been for him. Someone was expecting him to answer as he usually did, but he no longer answered. The calculation was wrong; instead of "one" there was "zero." That phone probably still rings occasionally, unless it's been disconnected. Someone is still counting on the likelihood that the receiver will be picked up and that the telephone will be answered. Not everyone reads newspapers.

And I'm counting on the likelihood that these letters will be saved on the disk: that I have lived and have spoken.

Amsterdam. I ought to be able to describe it, but what can I remember about it? Have I ever been there? There's no proof of it, no photo (I don't take pictures on trips; when I do, I leave the films undeveloped and throw them away after a few years), not even a train ticket in the side pocket of the duffel bag. I checked, because that would have helped refresh my memory.

And yet, I did look out of a train window. Yes, I remember exactly. There was a wide meadow divided into squares by intersecting ditches, which were full of water. There were cows corralled on one square. I don't know how they got there or how they would leave. I couldn't see a bridge, and they obviously couldn't jump over the ditch because they had grazed this square quite bare and it looked terrible, with yellowish green stubble interspersed with flashes of soil. The tufts of green were uneven, like scalp that was turning bald after an illness. One cow was up to her knees in the ditch and was hungrily chomping on grass closer to the edge of the water where it looked more nourishing.

Next came a clump of alder brush with leaves that glistened luxuriously in the sun, and then a fat man, sitting and fishing by the side of the ditch. He'd parked his small, white car right at the edge of the field. I wonder whether he caught any fish.

Anyway, that must have been Holland. I was utterly charmed by the plainness of the landscape. I must have looked out the window the entire trip, and I certainly returned by the same route, because I remember that I saw the same windmachine twice, or something like it, with wings. It was rusted and slanting and obviously no longer moving with the wind.

See, I'm starting to recall things. Now I do remember. I remember all too well! I even sent a postcard from there. Yes, it was a picture of a bicycle leaning against a bridge handrail, and I wrote on the back, "Greetings from a town where Europe bids herself good-bye to heave anchor and to go west or to East India, to Sumatra, to Celebes, to Tierra del Fuego, wherever." The main thing, to go far away. And yet she never leaves. The good-bye wave remains forever hovering in the air. The anchor sinks back with a rumble and this ancient Europe still sits there, in front of her brick house by the edge of the canal, where a few old chairs have been put out for the evening, and the view has turned a bit misty from beer or slightly hazy from some Far Eastern drug, which someone tried to sell me as soon as I got off the train. A musty smell rises from the canal. Leaves rustle on trees, and suddenly you're startled by the sound of a bicycle bell behind you. You jump to the side and he whirs by, one of those speedy apparitions in this town, grinning sweetly, probably on his way to the scene of some crime.

Exactly, to the scene of a crime! What else is there for those who missed the Great Adventure: a bitter regret that they can no longer go native or elephant hunting, temple raiding, and setting villages ablaze. This quiet but eroding bitterness drives them to crime, day by day. They're like sleepwalkers. They sit in front of their houses and drink beer, or, wearing ties, they go to their offices or walk with their children in the park. But if you suddenly call them, they fall down, reach for a pistol, throw a bomb!

I do remember the sweetness. We, Franz and I, were sitting by the edge of a canal. It was evening and the sun was shining along the canal straight in my face, making me drowsy and sleepy. The red wine we were drinking and the paprika-spiced food that made our mouths burn were having the same effect. The restaurant was Italian, and every fifteen minutes some clocks in a nearby bell tower played a long piece. This was a kind of vaguely melancholy tune which was almost, but not quite, a melody.

Franz had removed his dark glasses. It was an out-of-the-way place, and no one besides us was sitting on the patio. Even though the sun was shining in my eyes, I still saw that Franz was staring at me with this misty, self-demeaning look that I hate. I can't stand it. It's too degrading to be loved. Just then a waiter came to the table, a curly-haired, dark-eyed Italian boy, true to type. I looked him in the eye and he snickered as though we were sharing a secret. Franz's chair was at the edge of the canal. If I had stood up and given it a slight push he would have fallen in, flailing his arms. That's what I was thinking as I looked at him and smiled: how his arms would flail helplessly in the air and how he would fall into the water. And then how the Italian boy and I would kiss in the back room of the restaurant. How we'd divvy up Franz's money, because he had just put his wallet on the table. I didn't really want his money (but would the Italian have kissed without the money?). Wanting the money was really more to fulfill the expectation: to be a genuine and real East European, to finally betray the martyrlike trust that Franz had shown me.

Franz himself started on this topic. Emboldened by the wine, he started on his favorite theme, about hypocrisy and the relativity of moral values. He knew all about this, because twenty years earlier he had researched the topic as a young graduate student, had wowed students from good conventional families who had stared at him in openmouthed amazement.

A very conventional Dutch couple, middle-aged, dressed expensively but without taste, had seated themselves at the other table near the canal.

Franz said, "I'm sure that what they would really like to do is push each other into the canal."

Franz only had himself to blame, isn't that right, Angelo? I was thinking, Why did he have to choose me? at that restaurant by the canal as I studied him from across the table (squinting my eyes, as if because of the sun). This elegant, intelligent Franz, who was graying at the temples but who still had a youthful body that he exercised, scented, pampered, and dressed in smart, expensive clothes. It always reminded me of the mummy of that young pharaoh we had gone together to see at the Louvre. Why did he choose me as his victim when he could have chosen anyone, any beautiful boy or girl from among his students? I'm sure there are fools even today! But no, he chose me, an East European, because who else would have listened as reverently to his rebellious tirades? Who here would have given a hoot about his philosophy, which was based on delights of deconstruction, or about any philosophy, for that matter? Here, where everything has been discarded long ago! Even his most diligent students at Strasbourg probably thought he was a weird prehistoric creature and listened to his lectures only to pass exams, to get ahead in life, and then put their earphones back on and listened to U2.

And me? I never let him know that I had a Walkman and U2 tapes. That would have been much too painful for him. As a true East European I sat bright-eyed and listened to his outrageous ideas about freedom, about Foucault and Derrida. Why not? Especially for the promise of a delicious supper in the luxurious ambience of ancient Europe. I listened as a courtesan listens to her client, as a prostitute! All Eastern Europe has become a prostitute. From governments and university professors on, to the last paperboy, they are all ready to listen to wonderful speeches about democracy, equality, whatever you please, whatever the customer wishes! As long as he pays.

We're intelligent. We're not primitives! On the way back from Amsterdam to Paris a black man sat across from me, in a suit and tie, with a big belly hanging over his belt. He was very talkative, announced right off that he was from Cameroon and lived in Gabon (or was it the other way around?), that he was a businessman and had been to Milan, Hamburg, and Amsterdam and was going to Marseilles by way of Paris, and that he had lived in a four-star hotel. "*La vie est très chère à l'Europe! Très, très chère, ouh!*" he exclaimed, chortling and smirking in disbelief. It was supposed to be a lot cheaper in Africa and he planned to go back there fast. He looked out the window and expressed the opinion that Holland was a terrible dump, nothing but water everywhere. "There aren't any wild animals here, are there? It must be a poor country!"

In Brussels he wanted to open the window to take some pictures, so he could show them at home that he'd been to Brussels. But the windows didn't open in that train. It was air-conditioned. For some reason the air-conditioning had been turned off toward the end of the trip, and by that time everyone was ready to open windows. There was no air and it was hot.

No, we are enlightened. We know all about Europe. We have even read Foucault. We wouldn't be caught dead keeping our money in the legs of our socks like that black man from Cameroon or Gabon did. He had large square pads in the legs of both navy socks, and when he bought a Coke from the vendor he fished out a wad and removed a one-hundred-guilder bill.

We keep our money in breast pockets or even in banks. But all this doesn't help. I see East Europeans at the boardinghouse all the time, by the way. There are so many of them here, a wide variety, Poles, Czechs, Romanians. I can spot them from far away, and whenever possible I take a different path in the park or go into different cars in the Metro. They do the same, because East Europeans hate each other.

Anyway, I didn't push Franz into the canal. The bell tower played many times between the appetizers and the dessert. The wine went to my head. It was a 1986 vintage, and I thought about the spring of 1986 when those grapes must have been growing somewhere in Italy but when I was still walking in total innocence in an entirely different century, in an old rural cemetery, where tilting iron crosses and stone pillars slumbered among junipers and lilac bushes, with inscriptions such as I AM NOT DEAD BUT ALIVE (at the time I was trying to believe that I had faith in God's benevolence). That cemetery must still be in those boonies where from winter through half the summer the church is as cold as a grave, and where on Whitsundays birch twigs are brought indoors for the sweetness of their scent. I like to think that there are still people there today who worry about fodder for their cows and about their fishing boats, people who smile pleasantly as they accept money from Swedish tourists, as though they were doing a big favor, and so they are.

I can remember more: when the sun disappeared behind the houses and the water in the canal turned dark, the Italian brought some flaming ice cream to the table.

I'm not sure about anything anymore: is all this true? Did I really sit opposite that African from Gabon or Cameroon in the compartment of the express train and watch people on their knees on that amazingly flat field, pulling up tulip bulbs? And did the old woman in her colorful cotton skirt, hunched over and in a hurry, really go around the corner of the farmhouse to fetch green onions for the meal or to check that the hens weren't up to mischief?

Or was I one of them? Was I one of those kneeling under that blazing sun on the field, scraping the dusty earth with my nails?

The first landscape I remember, the one I can always give as proof of having lived, is actually more sky than landscape: a piece of sky with tops and branches of pine trees framed by a window.

Grandmother and I are sitting and eating at the table. The kitchen window is just high enough and the pavement just close enough to the wall that, although we live on the first floor, when we sit at the table we can't see the passersby on the street. Every now and then Grandmother complains, "Who was that?" She senses that someone has gone by, either toward Friendship Avenue or "toward the vegetable store," but she has not managed to crane her neck in time to see who it was. I have to get up then and look. "It was that Klauberk lady, Grandma." (Grandmother calls her "Old Biddy Klauberk," but I'm not allowed to call her that, even though that's what I think. On her mailbox it says SENNY GLAUBERG.) Or I say, "The fish lady." The fish lady is a lady in my opinion because she has a silver-fox collar on her jacket. Years later she will develop gangrene in one leg and it will be said that she sits in her wheelchair and drinks, "so that it won't hurt," and it's supposed to smell in her room.

When it's not Old Biddy Klauberk or the fish lady, it's "the Russian from below" or "an unknown person." The worst-case scenario is when Mad Milvi passes. She has epilepsy and may come in and announce that tomorrow is Palm Sunday, but it's better that she doesn't come in, at least in Grandmother's opinion, because she could fall down right there on the kitchen floor and start to foam at the mouth. That I would like to see, but otherwise Milvi doesn't interest me. I've seen her many times already, and she's always the same: puffy cheeks and thick black hair.

The sky that can be seen from the kitchen window is never one and the same.

Sometimes Grandmother puts her spoon aside and says, "Well, what do you see from there? What a bad habit this child has, always looking out the window during meals. Eat, your food will get cold and then you won't want it."

What did I see from there? It seems that I saw all the faces and landscapes of my life, and there was nothing for me to do but to see them again and to recognize them. Of course the food has gotten cold long ago, ready to be thrown out, but now there's no one to remind me of it. So I continue, as though I still had something to see or to expect.

Nor did I push Franz under a tram, although that would have been easy because the trams in Amsterdam have nothing in common with those primitive clattering trams in my hometown. In Amsterdam the trams are as ghostly as the cyclists. They appear around corners silently, give a signal at the last moment, and then slip across the bridge as if nothing had happened.

During nights in that hotel room I would awaken to hear Franz moaning in his sleep and grinding his teeth, and I knew I should feel sorry for him, that by just taking his hand I would calm him. But I could never bring myself to do that, because his unconscious suffering stirred me to feelings of aversion, as if it had been my own suffering. Revulsion prevented me from falling asleep. It was just turning light outside and blackbirds were starting to sing in the trees lining the canal, and someone was always shouting in Dutch on the streets. Someone crossing the bridge was laughing loudly, and someone was whispering right outside the window.

Only when the first tram signal sounded the beginning of day and the sun appeared did everything quiet down all at once. Even Franz lay still. Suddenly I was prepared to forgive him everything. The revulsion passed and was replaced by sleep.

What else do I remember? The sight-seeing boat gliding over the darkening waters of the canal. More accurately, the water gliding past the sides of the boat. The water and the peculiar houses that seemed to pass in a festive procession on either side. Their eaves were decorated with mystical figures, marble monsters or gods, still illuminated by the glow of the evening sky.

Then suddenly the boat entered the sea. Waves beat against the sides and the figures of gods were replaced by a wild and open sky. A huge wave came and washed us down to an underwater world, where we now are.

Or am I here alone? Was it only me the wave took along? Only I who disappeared into the silent depth, while Franz and the other people stayed swaying on the surface? Or was it he instead who slipped into the depth, leaving the world God knows where?

Where do I even get the notion that this Franz existed as a person? Perhaps he was an underwater figure? Strasbourg also has canals, and they are somehow connected with those in Amsterdam. I saw a ship in Amsterdam whose home harbor was Strasbourg. Maybe Franz decided to go home by a more direct route?

But no, he was more likely to have been an aerial figure, born from the air-conditioned air in the Palace of Europe. For me that's where he first materialized, handing me his card and urging me to call him in Paris on weekends. That's when he'd be there. Actually, I had seen him earlier, during the week. He had chaired the seminar for East European translators where I had been struggling with feelings of sleepiness, suffocation, and bouts of perspiration. I had been afraid that I would never escape from that horrible mausoleum, where ghosts in ties glided along corridors, plastic fish in an unreal syrup of power, the denser spots in an absolute rarefaction. One needed only to break the aquarium, to shatter the dome.

For me Franz was also one of those marginally real figures whose condition for visibility seemed to be an air-conditioned environment, that eroding gas which eventually dissolves flesh of all reality. Had I met him on the street I would have been startled, as though meeting a ghost. But I stuck his card into my pocket, and that fated him to develop bones and ligaments which I was fated to become familiar with through skin and flesh, like in an anatomy lesson. And I was to discover with amazement that a European, one of those flawless ghosts that hovered around me here, was nothing more than an ordinary, miserable, live human being.

And at some point he wasn't even that. At some point he would just be printer's ink in the morning newspaper, which was discarded as trash by the evening.

Today I lay on the bed half the day smoking and thinking about the kind of clothes I'd like to wear. The weather outside was cold and gray. The wind blew, and the branches of the ash tree swayed behind the window. The room was dark. I like this hotel, or boardinghouse. It's a place to disappear into. I may as well be at the end of the earth. Imagine, the chest of drawers here is mahogany. The bed on which I'm lying is also mahogany, with knobs and a headboard. This room could easily belong to the nineteenth century, just as I could easily belong in the nineteenth century. Hopefully the nineteenth century will soon arrive. Hopefully I won't have to wait long.

At first I thought about clothes from that period, but I couldn't really imagine much beyond the ones I'd seen at the movies yesterday. This mute woman had some kind of circular rib frame under her dress and a whole array of petticoats and bodices and I don't know what. It took her a long time to take them all off, and there was one scene where she was wearing all these clothes and the rib frame as she crawled in mud and lianas, trying to flee from a man.

Next I thought about fashionable summer clothes for myself—pale sea blue and coral-colored silk with coral-red buttons, pale linens, and glowing, blood-red silk embroidered with poisonous flowers. Always linen and silk, silk and linen! And sunglasses. The cologne would be Le Globe. That's not very fashionable anymore, but it's reminiscent of cypresses and rhubarb at the same time. And to go along with all this there should be a guy in sunglasses, with selfishly lusting lips, arrogant in his silver-colored sports car. I'd let him drive me to the Cannes Film Festival and there I'd drop him, despite his begging and pleading. There, there are bigger fish for me to catch.

Only the film festival finished yesterday. Anyway, I'm too late for that, and what would be the point of it all? The film I saw yesterday got the best film award or something like it at Cannes—*The Piano*. At the end the piano was lying on the ocean floor, in absolute silence. That reminded me of Franz or of myself, deep beneath the water, in complete silence. And in darkness.

Actually, Franz once bought me a silk shirt, silver gray, a fashionable color, but I don't especially like it—pretty standard medium-priced department-store stuff. At first I was impressed with everything in store windows here. Now I've come to realize that almost all is trash, garbage. In the windows on Rue Saint-Honoré you can see some quite beautiful things, but one vest there costs a fortune, and that makes you no longer want anything. I'd rather wear sackcloth or old Baltika-manufactured rags. The people I least want to look like are the East Europeans I see here. They buy themselves some horrible outfits on the Boulevard Saint-Michel and then prance about in them as if in seventh heaven! Even if they got hold of some Arabian oil sheik or some wealthy old émigré Russian Jewish lady who would dress them from head to toe in Versace or Rabanne clothes, I'd still recognize them, because they wouldn't know how to wear these clothes. Something would always give them away! Me as well.

Next I thought up some far-out clothes for myself. First I'd shave my head and pull on a big flaming-red wig. I'd put tiny round gold-rimmed glasses on my nose. My coat and pants would be dark green velvet, and I'd paint the nail of my second finger dark green to match. I'd wear a gold ring with a huge emerald. The collar of my dark purple shirt would be closed by a spider-shaped clasp of gold and diamonds. I'd wear boots with gold buttons. I wouldn't show myself during the day. In the evening I'd sit in the third row of the Opera, all alone, and I'd yawn insolently. I'd leave in the middle of the performance to pick up my lover in the Metro. He'd be a drug addict, thin as a skeleton, with huge black eyes. He'd probably have AIDS, but I wouldn't care about that. We'd still share the same needle.

Next I thought about a more practical dress, in case I lived with Franz, like he wanted me to. I'd wear it in that hallowed kitchen, and the automatic washing machine would always be washing it until nothing would remain. One day I'd go to the market to buy bananas, stark naked.

When you call me you always finish by saying, "*Je t'embrasse.*" That is, of course, when D. is not close by. You always say it as though you were really kissing me, and that is even better than an actual kiss. What's in real kissing, after all? But not everyone can say it like you do. I myself am amazed that I'm not at all jealous of D., whom I haven't seen, of course, nor do I want to see. Maybe I don't even love you. That's entirely possible. In that case, I love this not being in love. I want to talk to you. And that's what I'm doing. And in doing that, I slowly distance myself from the real world.

Many things have already become small and insignificant. I'm amazed how I could ever have assigned them such importance. Yesterday on the telephone you said, "*Je suis nul.*" I answered, "*J'adore ta nullité, Angelo.*" I said that this was as good as it gets. And after that we were silent for at least a minute. Not even the sound of breathing could be heard. As if the words had become reality and there were two nothings at either end. Can you imagine a Frenchman who could be silent for an entire minute on the telephone?

Angelo, I adore your nothingness. I'm sick to death and tired of all those people who are something.

Remember, I told you on the phone that I'd been to the museum. After I had thought about all those fashions and was becoming nauseated from smoking, I forced myself to get up (Grandmother would always say, "Well, force yourself to get up from there") and become active. I took a shower and dressed in that silver-gray shirt, which is not so bad after all; a colorful dark purple necklace would go well with it, the kind they wear nowadays, especially if one had a tan. I've been broiling myself by the pond in the Montsouris Park. There are others there, all sorts of flesh in the embrace of hot humid air. Sometimes I don't know which I find more seductive, a solitary jogger or the flowering tree that he's running past.

Next I debated whether or not to carry along my dark green briefcase, the one with the gold knobs, to give the impression that I was terribly official, was going to the library to take notes for my dissertation. Or to go empty-handed, as though I were available and independent, but my night of course would be occupied, don't even think otherwise! The briefcase was another present from Franz. He didn't have such bad taste after all, rather the contrary.

In this city everyone dresses to be observed—all except those recent arrivals from the real world, as you were, Angelo, and they are watched even more closely. Smiling that gently depraved smile of yours, you once suggested that I should get a little involved with voyeurism, as a sideline.

"*Les Parisiens, ils sont tous un peu voyeuristes,*" you said.

You needn't have suggested that because I've been involved with it from the moment I came here. For example, the Metro is very suited for it. Everyone there is spying on others, especially when the car isn't crowded. You need a certain distance. Yesterday, when I was coming home, a well-dressed young executive sat opposite me, a tall boy with wavy hair, insolent eyes, and full lips. I thought about how I'd kiss them and stared at him in a moment of absentmindedness. Just then he turned his head, bent his neck so that his lips touched the shoulders of his light green cashmere jacket, and with a rapid flick of his tongue picked up some imaginary crumb, just as animals, dogs or cats, do. He got off at the same stop as I and, carrying his briefcase, disappeared into one of the office buildings.

I finally left my briefcase at home but brought along some flimsy black covers, as if to hide important documents! In a word, I dressed to go to the museum.

To the museum! I wonder where I suddenly got that idea? I do after all have a free pass, so why not use it? I'm not a big museum goer, by the way. In my opinion, pictures in museums are all alike, and there are always obviously far too many of them. I think museums are almost as odious as department stores. The only difference is that you don't buy things in museums, although tourists with their cameras at the Louvre are almost as feverish as those shopping at Leclerc. What to take, what to leave?

Still, one can run into more relaxed characters at museums, and when they're examining paintings one can observe them without being disturbed. And often there are unexpected window niches where it's fun to sit down briefly to look out. So all in all, museums aren't bad. They're OK to visit.

In Amsterdam Franz and I went to museums. I distinctly remember one particular picture. It was something contemporary, a large canvas, painted completely full of red flames.

At the center of this fire a very realistic terrified rabbit was fleeing from a man with bulging eyes who was chasing it with an outstretched knife. The title was *Rabbit for Dinner.* Franz couldn't understand why I burst out laughing. I on the other hand couldn't stop. We were forced to leave the museum. I think he resented me for that, because he had paid for admission, after all.

But yesterday I went directly to the Louvre. Quite original, don't you think? I walked about aimlessly for quite some time and was beginning to tire. The seventeenth-century framed classical murals go on endlessly; so many torsos, faces, and motions, but nothing actually happens, just like on the street or in music videos, which I like to watch whenever I can.

In other words, I was starting to look for the exit (that's not as easy as it sounds; you can easily get trapped in there, just like in department stores) when I suddenly noticed a familiar face.

You may be familiar with *Gilles* or *Pierrot* by Watteau. I remembered it from way back. At one time a reproduction of that picture had been published in *The Children's Art Calendar.* It hung on the wall of our apartment for an entire month. I was already in high school then and was allowed to hang calendars above my desk. Grandmother hated that picture, but by that time she was already too ill and too weak to enforce her will. I would probably have obeyed her and would have turned the page, as if August had never occurred (yes, I'm pretty sure Gilles was on August). But now she just complained, "Why is he standing there like that, hands hanging at his sides? And what's the creature that's looking up from there, a wild boar? That's not a real painting!"

I actually sympathized with Gilles. We were like coconspirators, and I would very much have liked to comfort that boarlike creature. He had such an infinitely sad face. I even saw him in my dreams.

But yesterday I stood in the museum hall and waited until the crowd of German tourists dispersed from in front of that painting. A guide was explaining something to them, pointing to different details with a pointer. Interesting, what could he be explaining, I thought, the meaning of it all? They know everything and I still know nothing. Don't know the meaning of anything. There were several additional small, strange paintings by Watteau. Some were almost unpleasant, ugly and unearthly. One was titled *Indifferent,* a semifloating creature with an indefinable, dissipated expression. I was aware that long tracts have been written about this picture. I actually know quite a few things.

I finally managed to get to look at that *Gilles* in peace. I didn't really feel anything special. I had arrived somewhere, from an apartment in a prefabricated apartment house, which stank of Grandmother's medicines because no windows could be opened to let in air, to this city, to this picture whose copy had hung in that apartment. In that apartment I had actually dreamed that I would flee to Paris one day, would walk along the boulevards, would sit in cafés, would smile at people who would smile at me, and no one would be able to reach me there, not Grandmother, not the teachers, not my own life. Now I was here in this unfriendly city, full of tourists, suffering from heat, lying in my den until midday, not knowing what more to dream about. I could not even bother to dream about anything anymore. And I didn't escape from anything either. Everything came with me—my life, Grandmother, the stuffy apartment of my childhood, whatever.

Still, it's easier not to have a need to dream, for example, that someone loves me. At one time I dreamed about that obsessively. I didn't dream about anything else. And in the end, what was it all about? As Grandmother would say, only worry and misery. With time I'm beginning to see more and more how right she was.

Angelo, if only it would have been like this! If only I could really have stood quietly and hopelessly like this Gilles, hands at my sides, eyes wide awake. If only my inner recalcitrance and struggle would cease. If only this horrible mute bellowing would have stopped resurfacing from somewhere deep within me!

If only I would have been able to stand there and look at that picture with total indifference, the picture that once hung on the wall of Grandmother's apartment. If only I hadn't squeezed my eyes shut because I couldn't bear it all. Just as there, a hundred years earlier, always and forever there, in the high school lavatory where I had run to from class and closed and latched the door. Where I pressed my face against the painted green veneer, my mute face. I made no sounds in that stench. I scratched at the obscenities-covered wall, without knowing exactly why—the C grade for my essay, or the weird boarlike creature, or my own terrible flesh, or because Grandmother would die soon, or because my own ungainly limbs would someday have to take shape and become desirable, or, even sadder, because I'd become an adult and would do adult things, would betray and kill and forget, while at the same time I'd still be silently bellowing in that stinking high school lavatory at the end of the corridor, at the end of the earth.

As you know, I'm not really here to lie in bed, to wander around museums, or to write you letters I don't mail. I'm here to sit in the library, to read postwar French poems, to compile them into an anthology, to then translate it into a language this poetry cannot be translated into. An international foundation has given me a grant to do this, within the frame work of Past Philippini political intervention. I've done a little of this work, sat in the library and integrated. I've stared at the ceiling (actually there is no ceiling at the Beaubourg, there are pipes). I've stared at people, and also read some poetry. They wrote miles of poetry here during the postwar years and published it on beautiful thick paper. Bad, senseless poetry, simply gibberish that no one has been reading for a long time. Except maybe someone like me, someone else who gets paid to do it.

Still, a few very good lines can be found among the rest. Maybe all this work was written to obscure those few good verses, so that finding them wouldn't be easy.

Franz didn't understand how I could say that what I am doing is senseless. I suppose it really isn't. They pay me. It's my work. Franz had worked and sweated all his life, had read Nietzsche and Kierkegaard and Foucault, had explained all this to students, all about the inexplicability and senselessness of the world, in order that they would succeed in life. That was his work, which he must have performed diligently, otherwise he wouldn't have gotten as far, become a well-paid professor. Later I learned how to use this veneration of work to my own advantage. I would open up the collected works of some poet, turn the pages as if I were reading, and then I could be sure that he would leave me in peace and I would be free to think my thoughts.

Glory to work! Every morning on my way to school, as I sat squeezed between fat women on the trolley, I would pass that slogan on the walls of a factory. It is probably still there, because it was set into the brick wall when they built the factory.

Today, a thin, bespectacled woman, well dressed and fortyish, sat beside me in the library. She was reading Kafka, her brows wrinkled, her lips tightly pressed, making notes as she read. Her ballpoint pen flew over the white paper with amazing speed, and the sheets filled one after the other with careful, readable, delicate handwriting. She was working on her dissertation. I didn't once see her change her expression or look up from her work. At six she glanced at her watch, collected her Kafka notes, and went. The workday was done.

Of course, not everybody at the library is as industrious as she. Even today a girl who was sitting there, opposite the Kafka woman, was looking around, chewing her fingernails, looking angry. She put her head on the desk, closed her eyes, and heaved a heartrending sigh. Afterward I saw from her books that she wasn't from here, she was Russian.

How I love beautiful packages, clean streets, and the comforts of life! I love this world here, I even loved Franz and his meek work ethic. But then I would wish that hidden in the breast pocket of my improbable dark green velvet coat would be a tiny bomb, and that as I left the Opera in the middle of the performance I would forget it under the seat. The explosion would claim many victims.

But no, I don't really want to harm anyone. I don't want anyone to suffer. I want everything to vanish painlessly into the air, everything, department-store goods, paintings in the museum, the crowd that enters and exits the door, vanish like nothing at all and I along with that nothing at all.

Actually, it's good that I have my old men, those postwar poets. Yes, most of them have either died or, if alive, are as old as the hills. They still sit amid their books and keep writing. They spite their bladder disease and publish a new collection of poems every year, until death takes them as well. By the way, I've noticed that when they were young they wrote about death all the time, but now they don't talk about it anymore. You won't find a word about prostate glands, spleens, or atherosclerosis in their poetry. Those sources of suffering!

Still, they do help me pass the time. I sit in the library and drink desiccated poison from their ancient lips, hone my ears to catch the whispers of the dead.

And occasionally I do hear something, something that comforts me, that eases that constantly constricting leash around my neck; these few verses, for example:

> et des guitares hébétées
> se couchent tard
> entre l'amour et l'amitié*

---

*and the languid guitars / go to sleep late / between love and friendship—TRANSLATOR

I'm sending you these verses, Angelo, as a goodnight kiss, because it's very late. It's night and dark.

Sunday. That means that there's no mail delivery and there's no reason for me to go down to the mailbox. I'm not expecting anything, nothing at all really, not even my bank balance notice from the Société Générale.

Otherwise, I do go down there many times a day. The mailboxes have glass lids so that I can already see from the stairs if my box is empty. But I still go closer to be sure: empty. Then one day there may be a whole bunch of letters, from my mother, from a friend, the one whose hands once performed magic above the developing tank and whose handwriting I don't recognize, the one I had completely forgotten, although I obviously must have sent him a postcard from here, how else would he have gotten my address? For some reason letters like to arrive in bunches. God doesn't like regular distributions. Even pouring his spirit on the apostles was accomplished in one fell swoop.

At the very bottom there's yet another thick envelope, a long and strange letter from you, Angelo. I keep reading and rereading it, never tire of reading it. That's the advantage of letters we never receive.

Mailboxes . . . Who more than I knows the luscious titillation that makes my fingers tremble as they fumble with the lock on the mailbox, the lock on that temple of sin.

But now I should describe another landscape for you. This time it's neither a sky nor a bay, but a road. A road that leads to some mailboxes, beyond a barren hill, beyond maple trees, crossing under the sky.

By now I think I've mentioned a pair of hands several times, hands that once conjured the outlines of bodies and objects from noxious developing solution and white paper, and whose written lines I no longer recognize today. Those hands, whose movements once enraptured my glances, long ago, in a darkness that has since disappeared, belonged to a young clergyman. Yes, a minister, a black-robed man! Now you can understand my untimely allusions, my temporary eloquent sermonizing. It was all his, from there, from those times, that lost century in which I lived, which perhaps I most belong to.

That's where my adventure with religion all started, dear Angelo. Yes, it (religious adventure! loss of faith!) probably seems highly unlikely to you, and it is unlikely in this world in which all further appeals have become impossible. But there, in that frozen period of time, in that country behind the stacked firewood, the one from which I slipped away, it was still possible, even probable.

And I cannot remain silent on this, because this is a part of my crime. It's from here that the footprints lead to the mailbox, to the road that went by the maple trees, the one I promised to tell you about.

I remember that when I entered the church, it was cold, dark, and empty. Outside it was spring, and inside a gravelike frigidity prevailed. But this grave was not entirely empty. Some figures, wrapped in shawls, were crouching in the center pews. They were in the shadow of the tall backrests. That's why I didn't notice them at first. Were they dozing or were they dead? No, they moved, because someone moved up above, someone who had been kneeling at the pulpit and who now emerged and spoke in a somewhat hollow voice, "Now hear the words of God . . ."

A bony, winter-weary face, the collar of the clerical robe too large for the pliant, boyish neck, and that hollow voice, like the voice of someone practicing a speech in front of the mirror. Actually, he was talking to himself. He spoke to the dead whose pews were empty and to those few living whose dulled ears no longer caught the twitter of earthly voices, to those who opened their songbooks but no longer honed their hearing to the squeaking of the broken organ because their ears were already attuned to the song of the grave, the light seductive murmur of dust.

Then the one at the pulpit caught sight of me—a live being who had come from outside to penetrate his cold, peaceful chamber—and he lost the thread of his sermon.

In other words, I was soon sitting behind his back in the dark, inhaling the odor of his clerical sweat. And soon I was peeking over his shoulder to see the developing tank, hotly awaiting the miracle, the developing outlines of the miracle emerging from his hands.

You see, Angelo, from the beginning I have confused everything. I loved the hands of a human as if they were the hands of God, and I expected love from them, which was not human. I knew from the start that I was knocking on the door of the impossible, that it would never be opened, that the border was solid even though it might have appeared to be transparent, that the miracle would not occur. But I was enchanted, enthralled by the solitude, the pious senselessness that surrounded him in that icy church, in that deserted century from which all people whose legs could carry them at all had long since fled.

Besides, we conversed. At least I spoke. I needed someone who would listen to me. Honestly, I can't remember that he ever spoke. Was he even real? Yes, he was. He walked beside me and listened to me that summer and even beyond, when I, alone at last, passed the maples, crossed beneath the sky on the way to the mailbox from which I expected a revelation, some sign of salvation.

Those years now seem to have been my life's most beautiful. I was so totally convinced of my unhappiness and had the time to wallow in this unhappiness. I didn't have many other obligations. I had been forced to resign my teaching job, of course, because I had shown myself too frequently in that damp, stone-walled cave, that indescribable den of evil. Times were still like that then. But I didn't really expect anything of the world. The sweetness of my misery sufficed. Viewing myself as a victorious martyr, I exited the civil servant's office, and like an infatuated monk moved to an abandoned rural pastorate where the stone walls remained dank and cold throughout the summer but still failed to dampen my fever. I had to withdraw as far as possible, to as isolated a spot as possible, to oppose the world's oppression with my own; to be as far away as possible from the hands that changed liquid to pictures and wine to blood. My fever could reach its peak only from a distance; fever which I in turn transformed into words, faltering but steaming letters I wrote from that discarded pastorate, from that century that had since been declared wasted.

Those letters were my sweet sacrifice, my revenge on a world that always repaid me with silence. They were filled with the venom of jealousy. Because I was full of jealousy. I was jealous of his books, his clerical robes, the wooden figure of Christ whose poor wooden feet he so devotedly gazed on, even those hoary women between whose lips he inserted the consecrated bread during Easter Thursday communion, the thin insipid wafer whose floury taste has aroused me ever since, just as the taste of semen. I would have wanted to be the one and only surrogate for all those things, to have been the only one to taste that hopelessly unleavened bread!

That's how I discovered the mailbox for myself, the magic box with which one could easily transform the world into an imaginary place. Alone in an empty room I could put anything I wanted on paper. No force could stop me. As a final act, I would wipe my tongue across the strip of glue on the envelope, press my hand as the ultimate seal on the next sweet lie, and carry this heavy gift to the altar, to the counter in the post office, always covetously with my own hands, without ever trusting any mediators, least of all the mailman, who was a drunkard and could easily lose my precious message in the woods. I wasn't bothered by the possibility (totally likely considering my correspondent's occupation) that the letters would be opened and read in some office. Indeed, this increased the excitement.

And every evening I went on a pilgrimage to the mailbox, which was about half a kilometer from the pastorate. The mailboxes were by the side of the road.

For occasionally he wrote back, rarely sent a postcard or a few lines. But that was enough for me, because one condition for the gods' existence is the letters we write them, not their response to ours. Where is he now, the god of those times? I've heard that he's gone to America, but he may just as well have died, because I haven't corresponded with him for a long time now.

Now I correspond with you, Angelo. After all, I have to go through those motions which I learned at one time, have to follow step by step the road that I then contrived.

Maybe I'm confusing something? That was so long ago, the time and the distances have become opaque. It may be that I didn't even write him. It all seems too real. I may even have been married to him at the time I watched his hands over his shoulder, those hands which tried to endow wordly images with visibility. That would have been more ingenuous, although I don't quite know how that would have been possible. But as Grandmother used to say, who knows about those marriage problems, "Who knows!"

In that marriage, would I have been the man or the woman? Who's to say? Especially when dealing with clergymen and priests. What's really hidden under that clerical robe, the pious black gown?

I once tried on his robe, secretly, in the antechamber, and felt my body beneath it. I found this aroused me.

Anyway, those letters made me feel almost pregnant. During midsummer, in the evening when I used to walk to the mailbox, large fleshy cows, milked and content, would be ruminating by the road. Cumulus clouds that had gathered by the alder tree grove seemed to drip with a senseless desire, so much that it hurt. Swallows almost touched my hair . . .

Those trips to the mailbox were the only moments during the day that I observed the sky and sensed the heavens communicating with me about the beauty of unfulfilled expectations, the sadness of lengthy journeys.

As I passed them, I would observe the maple trees. There were three, and they stood rustling sensuously and ponderously, since autumn had not yet robbed them bare. Sometimes on August evenings I would stand beneath them in the warm dusk and let myself be enveloped by their rustling, so as to fully savor the pleasure of the pain.

As a lover Franz was wonderful. I think that's how it's usually put. Anyway, he wasn't one of those drowsy types we have in the North. I enjoyed sex with him; I was so wild with passion that I even surprised myself. And then, I started despising him more than ever. I don't know what it was, why I loathed him like that. His pathetic expressions, his hairy hands.

Sometimes on the street, in the Metro, I sense that I'm the object of a dark, hot Latin gaze, and then I yearn to be held by those hands, yearn to press myself against that hairy bestial chest. When that happens I usually assume an especially severe and impenetrable expression or, even better, hide behind my sunglasses. I had some sunglasses made at Lissac's, you know. Prescription glasses, because I'm blind as a bat without them, and now I love them. I can look right at those dark, moist eyes and see the gaze become confused, turn helpless as he sees me looking right at him but can't see my eyes. And then I pretend to continue reading.

But this is what happened to me yesterday. I went to look at the pictures at the Orangerie. There are a couple of small Matisse interiors there, you know, the one titled *The Boudoir*. The sunshine through the window has, over a long period of time, reduced the room's visibility to almost a nothingness. Faded it away, leaving only a couple of faint blue and pink lines, nothing more, just a breeze that billows the half-invisible curtains. I always wish I could be in one of those Matisse rooms, be that weightless figure of light, the one standing near the window of the boudoir, or the other, the one dozing, slumped in the easy chair . . . Oh, but I think I already wrote you about that picture. I'm starting to repeat myself, already!

I had been feeling happy for no reason since morning. When I exited the Metro at the Place de la Concorde, a shower had just ended. The square was still wet. Water ran into gutters. The sun came out, and the linden trees in the Tuileries gardens glistened luxuriantly. Their new growth was already quite high. Spring is over. Walking down the stairs in the direction of the fountains, I was thinking: how enormous the world is and how boundless its secrets! How boundless are my own secrets, let alone all that may still develop and become reality, and I wished I could live for at least a thousand years.

Have you ever been in the Tuileries gardens and observed how different the flower beds are? Usually flower beds in parks are full of large, showy flowers: roses, begonias, fuchsias, salvia. (Every summer around Saint John's Day, Grandmother would take begonias to the cemetery. Sometimes we'd keep them in the apartment briefly and I would secretly taste the sour petals filled with reddish juice.) But the flowers in the Tuileries are more like dry weeds: monkshoods, poppies, cornflowers, snapdragons, dwarf carnations, daisies, and such, just like those by the porch at Grandmother's half brother Ernst's place in the country. The flower beds in the Tuileries have probably been left there by mistake, remnants of that bygone, naive world, like the paintings by Renoir and Matisse, from the nineteenth century, from my world. They spread their bitter smell in the center of Paris. It makes you want to look around to make sure that the chickens haven't gotten into the garden, to give you a legitimate reason for chasing them.

A large black cloud appeared from the direction of the Place de la Concorde (hay sheaves should be covered with large plastic sheeting, which billows and glitters in the last rays of sunshine against the darkening sky). I fled from the park to take shelter under the archway of the Rue de Rivoli and watched the torrential rain and hail pelt car roofs. The wind tore loose a black sign from the wall of the Louvre and carried it high into the sky, a malicious harbinger of joy!

I had stopped in front of the window of an antiques store, and as I turned around I noticed a man and woman making a purchase just then. They were both young and unbelievably stylish, à la 1960s. The woman, actually the girl, had an innocent, powdered, doll-like face and artificially curled hair. One wide lapel of her tight-waisted jacket was decorated with plastic, fake-gemmed flowers. Her slacks were tight around the buttocks and flared at the legs, and she laughed gleefully as she spent the man's money. The man in his dark-framed glasses looked exactly like some innocent philosophy instructor from the Sorbonne, leaning toward Maoism but secretly enjoying the comforts of life.

Of course, everything there was terribly expensive, and I thought that a billion miles separated the people in that store from me. For them I was as distant as the begging Yugoslav war refugee who was crouching with her child by the column on the street. Knowing that made me even happier.

But I meant to tell you a story, not describe flower beds and people. The story, at least something resembling a story, happened later, after the park and the downpour. I went into a bar, one of *those* bars, because my feet were tired and I didn't feel like going back to my room yet. Not that the thought of a long, lonely evening frightened me. That doesn't disturb me anymore. But sometimes I enjoy observing the unhappy flesh that awaits its salvation in those bars. Besides, I wanted to toast the beginning of my new life. Yes, I had the feeling that something new was about to start, a departure, or something like that (of course, no sooner has one arrived than one realizes that every place is just the same as the previous one).

Sometimes when I have been in coffee shops and hungrily observed people, I've had the feeling that they avoid me like the plague. I dress properly and am not ugly, and yet if there is any room at all elsewhere, it has seemed that no one ever comes to sit at a table next to mine! Last night I didn't stare at people that much, only from a distance and nonchalantly, like at landscapes. If I smiled, then only to myself. When Grandmother used to beat me with the sewing-machine strap because I had talked back to her (we had an old Singer sewing machine, one with a foot pedal, that had been with Grandmother in Siberia), she wanted me to cry, but I never did. I would gnash my teeth together and think, I'm not going to die! Exactly that—I'm not going to die!—and that's exactly what I told myself as I lifted a glass of milk to my lips in that bar.

Yes, a glass of milk. You know, of course, that it's very fashionable to drink milk in bars nowadays, and I like that. There's something indescribably malicious in it; to lift a tall glass of cold milk, which costs fifteen francs, to your lips. That's a total escape from all those disgusting glasses of cow's milk that I was forced to drink, especially on the farm at Grandmother's half brother Ernst's place. Warm, just-milked milk! Flies used to buzz around the lukewarm burners of the stove in that kitchen! No, this expensive, sinful milk has nothing in common with cows or with anything that's supposed to be sensible. What a triumphant feeling I had as I drank it. Oh, they haven't vanquished me, not Grandmother, not Franz, not anybody. I'm the one who vanquished them. I'm not going to die!

That's when the man who was sitting at the table next to mine leaned toward me and said, "Please, would you smile for me?" I shrugged my shoulders and smiled. Why not? Have you noticed, Angelo, that people are often like that? If you're unhappy, then they run from you like from a mad dog, it's catching! But if you're happy and don't worry about anything, then you attract them like flies to honey, like leeches.

No, this Frenchman wasn't a leech. Quite a pleasant person in his mustard-yellow coat, Lacoste frames, and an expression that reminded me of a beaten dog—you know, a scar that couldn't be hidden by sunglasses or by the expensive clothes. Something had happened to him. Something in him had broken at some time, and now he was asking me whether he could sit at my table.

"Mais pourquoi pas."

Really, why not? I didn't care whether I sat alone or whether there was someone to talk with. His name was Jean-Claude, a good French name. I said I was Swedish. You know, I couldn't be bothered starting to explain where the country that I came from was, etc. When they hear you're from Eastern Europe they look on you with pity and speak with hollow words, as if you were a dead relative.

To this he replied that he was "*très européen*" and favored doing away with borders. I reminded him that right now they're starting to reestablish borders. (I enjoyed reiterating such newspaper stories.)

"Unfortunately, yes, but that will only be temporary; in the end I'm sure democracy and Europe will win."

He said this with a flat, sort of studied optimism. I felt as though I were talking to a child and should be careful not to say anything that might frighten him. Even a word such as "Amsterdam" scared him. He said they'd gone too far in liberalizing laws in Holland, because everything has sensible limits, after all. He ordered some more milk for both of us and asked me to remove my glasses.

"Veux-tu enlever tes lunettes?"

This sounded like a desperate assault, an attempt at assault. I did as he wished, thinking (and this thought made me want to laugh) that this is for the glass of milk, although I'm sure he didn't have the audacity to think that. And I thought further, how much does he think it worth for me to take off my clothes? But I took off my sunglasses and smiled at him, and he kissed me and I had no objections. He kissed me tenderly and his eyes were moist with desire.

In other words, he finally asked me whether he could drive me home. I knew what was implied, but I feigned naïveté and agreed with an expression that the question only implied the choice between the Metro and a car. In the street he kissed me again and tried to stick his hands in my pants, but then I suddenly didn't want it anymore. I withdrew and looked into his pathetic eyes once more, those that just a minute ago had aroused me. Now they made me laugh. I burst out laughing; he didn't understand when I said, You know, Jean-Claude, I have to go now.

"*Mon ami m'attend.*"

He looked like a child whose toy had been pulled from his hands. I felt sorry for him and turned to go, then I looked back; maybe I would have gone with him? But he had disappeared as if without a trace.

Oh, I felt so light, so on top of things! The night air was warm. I enjoyed breathing as I walked to the Metro station. There was a little time before the last train, and I was so happy that I was by myself and that I didn't need anyone. You know, Angelo, how sweet it is to leave someone and to run away.

Last night I dreamed of Grandmother again. In this town, so far from home, I have no protection from dreams. They're like houses with open doors: anyone can wander in, even those who are dead and obviously forgotten. I have obviously not forgotten Grandmother, but in yesterday's dream I saw a boy I used to love—platonically, of course—in high school. Actually, I myself wasn't even aware of it. In poems that I secretly wrote in my journal, which should still be somewhere, so that it could be checked, I'd write, "You, who don't love me . . ." and things like that. In my dream I was in bed with this boy, hugging him. It was exactly him. I knew it, although his body resembled Franz's a little, only slimmer. I don't think I've even thought about him for many years, and if someone would have asked me his name the night before, I wouldn't have been able to reply. But now I have the feeling that I've just seen him as a young, slight high school boy (he may already be a paunchy paterfamilias). It was so real, here, on this bed. As if everything I had ever desired is bound to happen, even if in a dream. I cannot die before!

Grandmother was also young in that dream, although I didn't know her when she was young. She was young, then suddenly old, and I knew in my dream that she was dead, and that was somehow disgusting. The entire dream was a little disgusting. A nightmare. Grandmother was showing me some kind of book. I wanted to see it in the worst way, but whenever I started looking at it, she'd pull it away because it was supposed to have lewd pictures. She said, "Whenever I let a man come near me, that sure made his day."

That, by the way, was how she used to talk when she was alive. She made me swear that I would never have anything to do with "such things." She used to admonish me to "keep away from women." "Once she has a child hanging on her, she'll start demanding money." I was surprised, because at the time I couldn't imagine what business I would have with women.

I think I ought to have a headstone made for Grandmother's grave. Maybe then she'll leave me in peace and not bother me in dreams. I've always intended to do that, but the money has always been spent before I've reached the stonemasons. She's buried in a cemetery on the outskirts of the city. In my opinion, it's a horrible place, masses of graves crowded under trees, each decorated with some kind of contraption, with withered flowers in water that's turned green and slimy in glass jars.

I even cried at the funeral. I felt so sorry for myself, for my miserable life, which seemed to have taken on a finality, a never-changing status. By the way, she wasn't my real grandmother. She was my mother's stepmother and had brought Mother along from Siberia. Mother was actually Polish or something like that. No one knew exactly, and Grandmother never talked about it. One story, which I remember from God knows where, was that Mother was actually the child of Grandmother's lover, only by another woman, a Pole who had died in Siberia. Maybe I thought this up myself, or saw it in a dream. Anyway, I don't know what my nationality really is or why I write these letters in this strange language. Sometimes it seems to me that I no longer understand this language. It seems so funny, so absolutely unimaginable! Really, I don't understand anything. How could I translate it into French? How to make myself understandable to you?

But then again, I have the feeling that I don't understand and have never understood any other languages, either, only that one. That's how I live, with only half a language.

I have tried to do everything just the opposite from what Grandmother taught me, at first out of spite, and then out of habit. I forgave her everything long ago, long before she died, when I held her frail, yellowed hand and she weakly squeezed mine, clung to it as though it could pull her back from death's door. Suddenly she was in my power. She was afraid of me, begging me, this onetime powerful and frightening grandmother. It was easy enough for me to forgive her!

But doing just the opposite, that was somehow ingrained in me by then. For example, we hardly had any books, and the only newspaper we subscribed to was the *People's Voice,* which Grandmother made me read out loud to her after I had learned to read. She pretended to believe what it said. I too was supposed to believe it. She hoped that this would ensure that she wouldn't be deported to Siberia again and that my future would be more secure as well. There were long, confusing sentences, which twisted my tongue and made me thirsty, words whose meaning I didn't know. But I liked Comrade Brezhnev. He was like a big, friendly grandfather with his bushy eyebrows, and I was always happy when he was off fighting for peace again somewhere in India because I was terribly afraid of war. Grandmother always said, "Come what may, the main thing is that we don't have war again." Her farm had been destroyed by a bomb during the war, and all her relatives had perished in the fire. Because

was heading for disaster. His lips were red from the tomato sauce. He stuffed the long, slimy noodles into his mouth and would probably have wanted to augment the sensual experience by my putting a hand in between his legs. But he didn't dare suggest that.

Today the weather is autumnal; the leaves on the ash tree behind the window are turning inside out in the wind. The tree is like an animal that's having shivers up and down its spine. In this kind of weather I'd like to eat apples and read novels, to put my teeth into the white flesh of the next apple (the entire porch would be filled with their melancholy aroma) and to avidly turn the pages in expectation of new murders. I really ought to close the porch door because it would already be cold outside, but I wouldn't bother. I'd just pull the wool blanket tighter around my legs.

I went and bought myself three apples from the Arab at the corner, one red, one green, and one yellow. It's ludicrous here. You get into a mood for something and you can make it happen. Just take five or a thousand francs from your pocket and you no longer know what to do with your life. I cut the red apple in half. It exuded a sticky, watery juice and a slightly stale smell. These are actually last year's crop. They have been stored for almost a year, and though they may look fresh, they taste of death. I'm thinking that apples that have been put in tombs with mummies must smell a little like this. Here they are even more advanced than the Egyptians in the skill of mummification. Here people don't even start to smell after death, because everything they've eaten is so clean and sterile. They take two showers a day and wash themselves with soap and water.

At least that's the impression I got from Franz, although I don't know what happened. His body stayed after I had gone. I let the door click shut and went straight down the stairs.

The aimless ringing of the telephone kept echoing in my ears. I went out, onto the street, into the air and the breeze!

In other words, despite the fact that they cost six francs ninety centimes per kilo, the apples I bought had nothing in common with those apples on the porch that I had been thinking of. If they reminded me of anything, it was of the apples that Grandmother sometimes bought before Christmas from the grocer across the street. There used to be long lines to get those, and people said they were "from Poland" or "from Hungary." Of course those had looked more shopworn, as if the mean-spirited women in heavy overcoats who waited in those lines had used them for pummeling each other to pass the time. Grandmother would always buy two kilos and put them on a tray with gingersnaps. Every evening she would halve one and we would eat it between the two of us. I would finish my half fast, but Grandmother would suck hers the entire evening, and my mouth would water. They had a slightly bitter taste and left a strangely tart feeling in the mouth, more like rowanberries, those Polish or Hungarian apples. No more would be bought all winter because they were expensive, three rubles a kilo, and Grandmother got seventy rubles pension per month. We had to live off that. Mother contributed sometimes, when she remembered.

I used to anticipate the day that the apples on the tray would be finished, because then New Year's break would be over and I would go back to school and wouldn't have to sit in our one-room apartment all day listening to Grandmother reminisce about her Siberian experiences. Those were always one and the same, five variations that she never tired of. I had to pretend that I listened to her. See, I even deceived you, Angelo. I seduced you with my devoted expression of listening. Actually, I may not even have heard what you were saying. I may have been examining your face instead, memorizing it. A person needs something to remember, after all. While pretending to listen to Grandmother's stories about Siberia with an attentive expression, I would simply be thinking about other things, for example: When would my mother come? Or how do people know what they are saying? Or, if I found a kitten, I'd hide it in the bathroom and would feed it until it grew big, and then there would be no recourse, Grandmother would have to resign herself to having a cat.

Occasionally Grandmother would catch me and slyly ask, "Now what was it I was saying?" And when I said, "Grandmother, about how that man wanted to kill you and make you into soap," but she had been talking instead about how they had been towed down the Lena River and those who had frozen to death had been thrown to the wolves, then an argument ensued: "You don't listen to me at all!"

In the end she would beat me, especially when I was stubborn and refused to apologize.

Now there is nothing to do with the apples I bought from the Arab. I'll eat them, of course. All my purchases fall flat. In stores I often start wanting things. Everything always looks so good in shop windows, on mannequins. But when I get home, it's nothing but junk. It's as if someone had exchanged it!

Instead, I recall some other apples. Cold, sensuous-smelling autumn apples, which I stole during my university days.

What all I remember now! I did indeed attend a university at one time, in a very small town by a river, behind the woods. The university had thick walls and a plastered ceiling. They taught astrology, graphology, and dead languages there. Usually it was autumn beyond the windows. Clouds that reminded me of intricate wrought iron would waft in the sky. The bell in the town hall tower would strike on the hour, and when people crossed the wooden bridge, it sounded ominously thundering.

In the evenings I too crossed that bridge. I too wore a long gray overcoat with its collar raised and a student's cap pulled over my eyes, because there was always a biting wind blowing along that river. I would walk fast, almost run, to distance myself from the terror of the university's disciplinary punishments, to crawl into the safe haven of my dormitory room in one of the dilapidated, tilting, brown wooden houses.

Behind this house were vegetable beds, with rotten potatoes, and some ancient apple trees. One of those grew directly behind my window. It did not belong to me or to the landlady. But at night it was easy to crawl out the window to feel for apples in the cold, wet grass, and then to quickly go back to examine one's find by the lamplight.

There I ate those apples. I had no money with which to buy any from the store. I read Dostoevsky and stopped going to class. In the end I started having dreams about an angel, every night, a slim, black angel who just stood at the foot of my bed and did nothing else. That vision was so unearthly yet so sweet that I wanted nothing more. Ever since, I find the smell of apples arousing.

The dean finally started looking for me, and I went back to attending classes. But I no longer understood what was happening. At one point I started to cry during a lecture because I was thinking about Count Myshkin. Angelo, did you ever read *The Idiot?*

As you can see, nothing actually happened in Amsterdam, nothing remarkable, anyway. I simply spent a few days there at Franz's expense, gradually hating him more and more. An ordinary, mundane deception which wouldn't warrant even a mention in the newspaper or any words at the damnation on Judgment Day. After all, Franz was involved in it all just by chance.

One's day-to-day life involves constant deception, after all. I live a life that doesn't interest me, say things I don't believe, spend money that isn't mine. Who does it belong to, by the way? Who owns my life? To whom has it been pawned? To heaven or hell, to the European Bank for Development and

Reconstruction, about whose dubious machinations Franz so enjoyed talking?

You know, I have the feeling that just as I'm spending money that doesn't exist, I'm living a life that doesn't exist. My actions, my days, are only make-believe, and yet they continue. The automated teller at the bank does not refuse me money. It just whirs for a few moments and a hundred- or a two-hundred-franc bill appears between its jaws. I pull it out before it changes its mind, and leave, like a thief.

But sweetbrier is blooming in Montsouris Park right now. A young couple had themselves photographed by the sweetbrier today. And tulip trees, there are two tulip trees by the pond. I had read the name earlier in some books and had imagined something grand and festive with huge red tulip blooms. Actually the flowers on tulip trees are quite small, greenish white. The tulip tree's Latin name (on a green metal sign) is LIRIODENDRON TULIPIFERA.

The strange thing is that I don't want anything. I don't need anything or anybody. I don't miss anyone, even you, Angelo. Of course, the reason I don't miss you is because I talk to you all the time; I probably couldn't do that if you were here.

To me, the notion that someone is missed, that someone's proximity and services are required and demanded by someone else, seems horrible and sinister. It's so good to be alone. Not to talk nonsense with anyone, to sit by the pond in Montsouris Park and to observe the voiceless birds, ducks and geese who do their thing, twist their necks and hiss angrily over pieces of white bread.

I like to prowl in out-of-the-way places where few others wander, for example, the hall at the Louvre where they exhibit pictures of the museum's history. Hardly anyone ever goes there except a guard who sits there and a crazy Englishman who carries a copy of *A Walk in the Louvre* (London, 1993) and is studying the exhibit. Americans storm past there in droves. The same goes for Russians, Poles, Japanese, and

Czechs. To see the Mona Lisa! And why not, quite a beautiful boy!

I once prowled in the history hall. They have great pictures there, for example, a painting titled *The Reopening of the Great Hall* (1947). That looked familiar. It was similar to pictures in my onetime history book or in a book of colored photos I had looked through once in a schoolroom of that ancient country.

Some kind of cardboard optimism, fake and genuine at the same time, made people from that postwar era all look somewhat alike, wherever they may have been. This is probably considered embarrassing. I hadn't seen pictures like that anywhere in a long time. They must be kept in storage somewhere, waiting their turn, those red-cheeked survivors of 1947 who seem to be saying, "Well, enough killed. Now let's taste some of life's other pleasures."

Tell me, Angelo, whisper in my ear so that no one else can hear, doesn't history give you the creeps? Not just that throats have been slit, and are still being slit, but that this is of absolutely no consequence, that man will put up with immense suffering, immense!

By the way, the linden trees in the Tuileries gardens are in bloom right now. Only the bees are still missing. Someone had even collected linden blossoms. A bench had been dragged under the tree, and there were footprints on it. The blossoms collected in a paper cone had been discarded in a nearby trash bin. Maybe this person simply had the urge to pick blossoms. It may have reminded him of something, of some other time, or of the story "The Collection of Linden Blossoms."

Another thing I like is personal museums. These are also seldom visited, and in such museums the dead person's belongings are so peaceful! Books lying "opened" on the desk are no longer disturbed. No one moves the china elephant to the left of the china Virgin. Her place is on the right. There may even be a little garden or empty yard behind the window. No one is ever there. The dead person's view must not be spoiled. If there were anything in the yard, then maybe a child's toys lying deserted on the grass, yellows and pinks. Only the clocks would still tick. A somnolence always comes on there. One would like to lie down on the bed that looks as if it had just been made, although no hand may have touched it for weeks. But one can't, there's a rope pulled across the doorway.

Remember, we talked about house museums on the telephone. You spoke about the Thomas Jefferson museum you had visited in your home state, Virginia. You told me Thomas Jefferson's bed was in an alcove between two rooms. There people could say they slept in either room, fell asleep in one and woke up in the other. The bed was right on the border between the rooms.

At first I was totally enthralled by Franz's Paris apartment. It was on Île Saint-Louis with a view of the river. Can you imagine! The European Union paid generously for his living quarters in Strasbourg, and he lectured in Paris as well.

"This apartment is the only luxury I allow myself," he told me.

That was a couple of days after we had returned from Amsterdam by separate trains (that had been Franz's suggestion) and after Franz had been to Strasbourg. We were walking along the little street that halves Île Saint-Louis lengthwise. A store was still open, and there a dead pheasant was hanging head down, its colorful feathers glistening by the glow of the lamp. The storekeeper stood by the counter rubbing his hands; he seemed happy to have such a bird.

The door of the house was big and heavy, like a church door, but it closed behind us with a quiet click. The inside was totally dark; only the red signal on the light switch glowed like a wolf's eyes, and I had the feeling we were being trapped in a box and the lid had been locked with a click! I hurried to the switch and turned the light on. The thing I fear most is being trapped, having no way out.

We went up a wooden staircase to the fourth floor. The steps had a flat polish and creaked. Franz opened the door with two keys. The locks were well oiled and turned easily. We slipped in and there we were, at the place the crime would occur.

By the way, it's strange that neither that first night nor during the entire week that followed did I ever meet another soul in that stairway or corridor. According to Franz, the concierge lived in the adjacent house. I don't remember that I ever heard any sounds from the other apartments; only the fact that the garbage bins filled up indicated that there must have been other people living there. But I didn't pay that any attention *then;* I'm used to places in this town that are deserted, seemingly too soon and too fast. But later I thought about it and came to the conclusion that it was likely that no one ever saw me come or go. Just as though I too had become prematurely invisible in that soundless house!

Franz's apartment was actually one large room. The kitchen formed its own spacious niche (but I've already described the kitchen for you) and the bathroom was separate, of course, lined in black tile, decorated with golden sphinxes, pharaohs with their wives, and lotus blossoms.

The room was very high. A wooden balcony had been built at one end, a mezzanine, with the bed and more bookshelves, in addition to all those which covered the lower walls. A staircase led to the mezzanine, and if one stood at a certain point, one could only see the water in the river, where clouds would be swimming during the day, or the next, or the next to the next day.

That night I went up and down that staircase many times. I adore living quarters with staircases. There's something dramatic about them. In the theater someone often descends the stairs in a robe or with the hem of a gown trailing down the steps, stops halfway, with a hand grasping the handrail, and says something that breaks the scene. For example, "There he is." Or "I've had enough!" Everyone on stage starts to move and to complain, but the hero remains immobile on the steps and observes the goings-on from an elevated position, because it's always the hero who descends the staircase where he has formulated his sinister thoughts. The maid never comes down the stairs but always through a door deep in the stage, or just from the side of the stage, to announce that dinner will be served.

Franz came from the kitchen and in a hollow, theatrical voice announced, "*Madame est servie!*" He was picking up on the role-playing because I had just come down the stairs and said in an equally cavernous voice, "Death stalks this house— open the windows!" We were wild that night, as if in a fever, and the wine we drank raised the fever to an even greater pitch.

Can you imagine, Angelo, I have always dreamed of glass furniture. Franz had a table, a bench, and a column, all made of glass, and the foot of the column was made of a spiraling column of glass discs. I found fingerprints on the glass and took a paper towel from the kitchen to clean them off, because glass has to be spotless. Then I found some more and I rubbed and polished, and Franz couldn't understand what was wrong with me. Until I realized that one can't get glass like that clean. As soon as you touch it or put a plate with food on it, it smears again.

People shouldn't live in houses with glass furniture. That made me sad, and I lost my good humor. I threw the paper towel into the garbage bin and pressed a huge handprint on the glass tabletop. Then we went to bed, because what else was there for us to do?

Grandmother used to curse whenever they cheated her out of ten kopecks at the grocery store (at least she thought they had cheated her) or when the bums shouted at night on the roof of the house next door and threw bottles down on the street so that shards scattered: "The end is near, the end is near, what else!" I once asked her what "the end" was. She said, "The end of the world." She didn't explain further, only ordered me to read the *People's Voice* out loud for her. There they talked about the struggle for peace, which Comrade Brezhnev was carrying out in India or some such place, and that reassured me because the end couldn't come while we were firmly marching on the road to peace and progress.

But there were times when planes flew low and the house would shake and a terrible bang would follow somewhere. Or it would suddenly turn dark outside, someone with a terrible voice would curse in Russian on the veranda of the opposite house and someone would push garbage bins over with horrendous clattering. Then I'd squeeze my eyes shut tight so as not to witness the end of the world.

After a while I would have to open my eyes again, because how long can you keep them shut, and I would find that the world was no more ended than before, that it continued as deviously as ever. Potatoes were still being sold at the vegetable stand across the street at six kopecks a kilo, "but half are ready to be thrown out right away." The sun had emerged, and overweight women in flowered polyester dresses, shopping bags in hand, were marching toward the trolley stop with determined expressions.

I often dreamed that it was war, like in the films we went to watch with the class. I'd be crawling under shells and everything around me would be burning. Finally a shell would strike me, and I would wake and listen to whether Grandmother was breathing or was dead. Sometimes she breathed with a whistle and snort, but other times so quietly that nothing could be heard. Then I'd creep to her bed and think that she was dead, that everyone was dead, and that I'd been left totally alone in the world. But up real close you could see she was still breathing. Bad-smelling breath came out of her mouth.

Sometimes that wasn't enough to ease my mind. I'd start thinking that the world had ended after all, but they were hiding it from me, that Grandmother wasn't my grandmother at all, that my classmate Alo wasn't my classmate, that even Mother wasn't my mother, that they were all witches (that's exactly what I thought, they were witches), and that they only made believe I belonged with them. Then I'd cry under the covers because I'd feel so sorry for myself. I alone had survived in a world that had ended. I felt even sorrier for the poor world, which didn't even exist anymore.

One morning I spoke to Franz about this. We were in bed and the sun was shining outside on the Seine. Reflections from the water were jumping around on the ceiling. We could hear the constant noise of the traffic on the opposite shore. The smell of the river—and even more intensely, the bitter smell of car exhaust—entered through a window that Franz had opened earlier. The bells of a church on the island were chiming, but they were barely audible. A ship passed on the river and threw the jumping light reflections into a total dither.

Franz listened to me quietly and then said that he had had almost exactly the same thoughts as a child. Even later, when he'd been a first-year student in Paris in '68, he'd pulled up stones from the ground, had seen cars burning, and had enthusiastically thought that the end of the world was really coming. But no end had come, not the world's nor anything else's.

I pressed myself close to Franz, and it seemed to me that the entire house was drifting downstream with the river, that we were the only humans in that house, and that soon we'd come to a waterfall or to the sea.

At coffee Franz talked about the idea of an end, and the hysteria associated with the end of the millennium. Europe would not be experiencing it for the first time, but one couldn't reconstruct the thoughts of people who had lived in the years 999 or 993.

I don't know whether one could even find out what a person sitting on the Metro is actually thinking as he travels through the underground, both hands tightly clasping the parcel on his knees, on his daily way home from work.

You know, Angelo, I have always been overwhelmed by the beauty of the world, wherever I may encounter it. I have never been able to resist it! It could be just a passing glimpse out of a train window, the most ordinary little path that meanders along vineyard-covered hills, or yellow tea roses dropping petals as they lean against the fence of the railway station, some ordinary street corner with its Bistro sign, or the bound volume on the counter of some bookstore. And people, the way that they can be fiery and ethereal at the same time! Poor me, I'm totally incapacitated by this. Strength drains from my limbs. My arms become weak. Just as when I saw you for the first time, Angelo, I was immediately overwhelmed by your beauty.

The maid just came. Every morning around ten-thirty, her quiet knock sounds: knock-knock! She's always cheerful, this pert black woman. "*Bonjour, Monsieur! Maintenant, ou tout à l'heure?*"*

Right away, why not; meanwhile I can read yesterday's *Le Monde* in the lounge downstairs, something about Bosnia-Herzegovina, about AIDS, about the alarm caused by the turn of the millennium, hunger or war that has besieged different places around the world.

When I return to my room, the floor is still damp. It's not painfully clean, by the way. Grandmother would have called this kind of floor washing "licking"! Floors were supposed to be washed down on one's knees, not with a mop at the end of a broom. Still, following the black woman's visit, the room seems to be flushing from cleanliness. There's a fresh newspaper in the wastebasket ready for new trash. The chest of drawers has been dusted.

---

*Good morning, sir! Now, or in a little while?—TRANSLATOR

And the bed! Even if I would dedicate all my strength and energy to the task, I could still never get the bedcovers as smooth. It's as if no one had ever slept in the bed, or lived in this room! One immediately gets an urgency to wallow in it, so that such pristine surroundings won't make one feel too unworthy.

I now understand that servants are more for looks than for comfort. Today even the rich don't have many servants. Instead of beauty they prefer simplicity and functionality in life. Healthy teeth in preference to diamonds, safe cars rather than rare marble. But people in the seventeenth century had no choice. There was little they could do about aching teeth and death, and so beautification became the only virtue in their disappearing days.

Take, for example, gold, silver, and gems, or silks and velvets. Today these are hardly even valued, but I've seen the French royal treasury in the Louvre. There, there's an entire collection of dishes carved from semiprecious stones. I can't even imagine how they were crafted. They have been hollowed out of single pieces of stone, with walls so thin that occasionally rays of light gleam through veins and lines in the rock formation.

For example, there's a chalice made out of dark green nephrite on a gold pedestal decorated with rubies; amethyst jugs resembling clusters of lilac blossoms on June evenings; dishes of rose- and gray-streaked agate; jugs from different-colored jaspers, green, dark red, and a yellow resembling murky river water; an inkwell from silver-speckled black jasper; decanters carved out of large crystal blocks; a tray of dark blue lapis lazuli on a gold pedestal . . .

Also the earrings belonging to Empress Josephine, huge tear-shaped pearls; or the jewels of Queen Hortense and Queen Marie-Amélie, covered with dark blue sapphires. Not to mention the huge diamonds, which are transparent but brilliantly blinding at the same time, preventing any entry into the glittering worlds hidden within them.

There is no entry to them anyway, because all these jewels are in glass cases, hopefully even in bulletproof glass cases. At one time they belonged to someone. Now they're called national treasures. And really, who would drink the vineyards' gift from those nephrite chalices? Who would dip a pen into a jasper inkwell? And then, what words would such a person write?

But I think those glass cases will soon be smashed because the temptations of beauty have not disappeared. And those nephrite, jasper, and crystal dishes will also soon be smashed.

You know, there was not much beauty in the country from which I came.

One of those I loved there, a poet, an unwell man, half mad and crippled, who shuffled for shelter from one stranger to the next, even he has said "It is not beautiful" about this country.

But yet, when I walked along the road by the fields, past the maple trees, past the mailboxes, across the highway, and even beyond, past the next field where the road submerged into the woods, among the spruce (on October days it was semidark there, and one could smell the aroma of mushrooms touched by frost), even beyond the spruce forest, along some deep muddy ruts, until the path became sandy and rose to a plateau where a pine forest began, up to a small clearing, actually a flat spot where the pines were sparse, which was covered with dense level heather, and which traces of sun still reached on autumn days, I would always stop on that spot, with my feet in the sand—like the pines—and I'd think, How magnificent this world is!

But then another thought would come, to shadow, to darken, that first thought: The end of the world. Oh, I would have wanted to put my arms around his neck in this clearing, to hold him, to protect him, to shelter him with my slight body over his, just as I would like to shelter you, Angelo, only my arms are so short!

I couldn't resist the temptations of Franz's apartment, the glass furniture, the book spines, the slender crown of the poplar tree, which constantly shivered in the wind behind the window.

When Franz suggested that I stay there while he was in Strasbourg (and that week he had to go to Geneva as well), then I finally agreed, even though initially I had protested, because I knew right away that no good would come of it. I had a foreboding of doom and tragedy.

You must never stay in places you find tempting—where the world's beauty is stalking to ensnare you in its glittering trap. These one should only pass through or pass by, pretending disinterest. As soon as you pause, you are lost. Then the switches are already in the brine. You have succumbed to temptation, and temptation always leads to crime. The world's beauty is always baiting to be destroyed.

But here they already know how to set traps. They are masters at this. Every common fruit merchant knows how to arrange his oranges so that they leave the impression of holding the key to all of life's pleasures!

So I stayed on in that apartment. Franz went to Strasbourg and to Geneva. It was a dream week! I didn't go to the library at all. Some days I lay on the bed in the mezzanine and browsed through books, half asleep, napping occasionally, waking occasionally, the distant sounds of the city in my ears, sleep at times withdrawing, at times approaching.

For example, I remember a dream that was totally realistic and took place in that same room. The doorbell rang and I opened the door to a turquoise-eyed beggar. I prepared fried potatoes for him and cut up some pickles to go with them. On eating, he was grateful, but still very dignified. Then he looked at me with his blue eyes—this time they were dark blue—and, smiling sweetly, said, "It's nothing, we're all mortal."

Now where would I have found potatoes to fry in that apartment? There were no potatoes there, not to mention pickles. Did I even live in that apartment, or was it all a dream? In that case, the dream was too long and too realistic. I remember the view on the river, the kitchen, the dead pheasant that hung in that store with its colorful wings spread.

I awoke from that nap strangely jaunty and ready for

action, and I stormed outside. I wandered along the streets. Sat in a café, but only long enough to drink a glass of water, and continued down to the water's edge. Pushed my way amid the crowd flowing down the Rue de Rivoli and ran into a museum. Concentrated self-consciously on the subject matter of some hyperactive painting, trying to identify the figures according to the explanations given in the sign on the wall next to the painting: the emperor, the empress, the mother of the empress, the pope . . . running past the next pictures without actually seeing anything.

At one point when I was running around like this, I happened on a group of my countrymen. I recognized them from a distance, even before I heard them talk. They were standing in front of the window of Samaritaine and were criticizing the display, while secretly lusting for it, lusting for all the merchandise and wealth that their poor eyes were seeing for the first time.

Actually it was I who was standing there, looking at the window display. You know, if you've ever stood in front of those windows, you may pretend that you're above it all, but you'll stay there forever. But it's too pathetic, too meaningless, to write about. One ought to write only about things that have at least a smidgen of literary quality, a trace of noble suffering, not about East Europeans dressed in jogging suits and running shoes, stopping in front of the opulent window displays in this city.

In short, I fled from them. I turned down a side street and almost ran, to avoid seeing myself in front of a store window lusting after those rags. I had no idea about the direction I was going, but suddenly I found myself on Rue Saint-Denis, where the air is thick with the smell of burning oil and charred meat. There they sell hot dogs and hamburgers every few steps. That's where the prostitutes hang out.

I like those girls. They stand absolutely still. They don't hassle, don't knock on windows like in Amsterdam, because they're forbidden to proposition clients. It's strange. She stands there, a man comes, they make a deal, and later she stands there again. It's a challenge, an insult to any idea of time passing, to any idea at all. Oh, I feel for them; after all, I am one of them, though they wouldn't accept me as such, not even they.

Aware of where I was by now, I continued along Rue Saint-Denis, without any idea where I was heading. I had no intention of going anywhere, but when I saw the door of a church open to the street, I stepped inside. It was unintentional, simple, just a place to take shelter. The smell of charred meat was making me nauseated.

Believe it or not, there wasn't a soul in that church. It was completely empty. The sun was slanting through the highest windows. There were cane-bottomed chairs, cubic meters of silence, and a smell like that found in houses that have been uninhabited for a long time and that no one intends to return to.

I recognized this smell. One spring I had gone by the road that I wrote you about, through the woods and beyond, until I came to a clearing where a deserted house stood. It was without windowpanes or doors, a gray log farmhouse, very typical of those parts. I went in, and there was the same smell. The fire under the stove had not been lit all winter. No one had looked out the window or noticed that a blazing sun was riding in the sky, throwing sparks across the heavens, and that everywhere young green blades of grass were pushing up through the earth. A terrifying hymn to life was rising deafeningly through the previous year's fog.

Inside it was damp and dark. The roof had leaked, but the walls were still standing. Soon they too would fall prey to the grass. And the silence. The screaming of birds, high in the sky, reached there only as a faint echo.

I stood at the window of that deserted house and looked out on the blinding day, which was a thousand miles away, and there, very far, went I, young and lithe, my lips red, my clothes white, through green grass until I disappeared between the birches.

The humidity is terrible. My shirt is sticking to my back. It's impossible to concentrate. It's threatening to rain at any moment, to thunder. But nothing happens. The sky remains hazy and tree leaves glisten heavily.

It's Sunday today, and I went to Versailles. It was stuffy on the train. I don't know why the windows in these trains don't open. The palace courtyard at Versailles was like the bottom of a stewing pot in which some exotic dish was being cooked from a mixture of Japanese, German, and East European tourists. I went with the flow, through the palace, through the king's bedroom, and through many other empty rooms. Pictures hung on walls and people traipsed through, all with the same facial expressions, earth and stones. And outside, beyond the windows, the fountains sprayed water toward a pale sky in the stifling heat.

I didn't even go to the park but fled in the opposite direction, along the tree-lined avenue that goes through the town. There it was shady and empty of humans. Only in one place some men were playing *boule*. The balls fell with dull thuds and always raised small columns of dust, which remained hovering in the air. These men were big and sturdy. When a solitary woman walked past them through the sunshine on the street, they ogled her and laughed among themselves.

Angelo, why on earth did I stick my nose into the world of humans? I ought to have stayed where my place was, in the world of plants, in Eastern Europe, in the stuffy apartment of my childhood where Grandmother's plants luxuriated on the windowsill.

As soon as humans and their desires come into play, only trouble and misery ensue. I followed Franz because I wanted to see what it would be like to be human, to live like a human being. That was my terrible crime that won't be forgiven. I went along with the game, but passively, without believing in it. And now see what happened! Sometimes when Grandmother was irritated by my helplessness, she muttered, "Oh Lord, there's no way this one will survive!"

And I didn't. Grandmother was right in everything.

. . .

Serious things make me laugh. For example, when the water is turned off. Once in that apartment with the glass furniture there was no water; Franz was still at home. It may have been Monday. It turned out that everyone had been notified about this in advance. A repair had been scheduled and that's why the water was turned off, but Franz had thrown the notice into the wastebasket without reading it. No one reads all the junk that arrives in the mail. When I was alone, I read almost everything—only the pamphlets, of course. I didn't open envelopes. Those pamphlets peddled all sorts of goodies, trips to various islands, castles in the mountains, insurances against every imaginable accident . . .

In short, no water came from the tap, just a dry, gurgling sound, and Franz totally lost his cool. He had been ready to take a shower. He started telephoning and demanding that the water be turned on right away. He called at least five different places before he found the one who explained the problem and told him that the inconvenience would be corrected in three hours, at the latest. Sorry to have caused a problem.

This amused me no end. I told Franz that at one time, in that other country, in the little town by the river, I had lived for three years in a house that had no indoor plumbing, that water had to be brought in with a pail from a tap in the yard. The pails were soon covered by a layer of rust from all that water.

Franz looked at me with an angry expression. He had already settled down and knew what the problem was, but he still couldn't take a shower. He looked at me as if I were intentionally telling him this to irritate him. Suddenly his face lit up. He had discovered my lie.

"But the toilet, how did you go to the toilet then?"

In the yard behind the house, I explained, and that I had only learned to use a water closet here. That at first, when all the water came in with that terrible roar, it had frightened me!

That seemed to excite him. I became a stinking primitive in his eyes, someone he had caught in the jungle and tamed. He wanted to drag me into bed and was much more callous than usual, and I found this sudden show of meanness arousing.

Actually, of course, the toilet in Grandmother's apartment did have running water. It was a recently built prefabricated complex. I enjoyed sitting there, and I used to go to the toilet even when there was no need. There it was warm and quiet. The outside world was far and removed. One could latch the door from the inside with a hook. One couldn't stay there too long, though, for then Grandmother would become suspicious and come and bang on the door: "What are you doing in there so long?"

I've had a weakness for clean white toilets ever since. It's so safe there. All signs of life have disappeared, as if by magic. Not even smells remain. One doesn't think about bloodletting and butchering there. The unfortunate people of the seventeenth century had no such safe havens. In Versailles I didn't see one toilet or shower amid all those bedrooms. Louis XIV couldn't even dream about modern conveniences. Fleas and filth pestered the contemporaries of my dear Madame de Sévigné, the same for Madame de Lafayette, who was always sickly, and for the somber La Rouchefoucault, who often tried to entertain the sickly one.

But as to the rust-covered pails, that was true. I didn't lie to Franz about that. As a student in that university town with the wrought-iron-like clouds, I did live in a house where the privy was down the hall and the stench made my eyes water. That stench stuck to clothes, and sometimes even now I seem to smell it, even though I discarded all my clothes from those days long ago.

The evening brought relief after all. A few drops of rain fell with a rustle on the leaves of the ash tree. The shower never materialized, but the wind turned cooler and I decided to ride to the center of town to walk by the river. After that week on Île Saint-Louis I've developed the habit of walking near the lower docks in the evenings, near the edge of the water where the wind blows along the river and poplar leaves rustle overhead. In the dark hardly a soul is there and I don't run into people, not even lovers kissing. Sometimes seeing them makes me sad. I wonder why.

Now I'm back from my walk. My feet are tired but my head is clear. It's past midnight, but I'm not sleepy and will write you a few more lines, to take advantage of this short respite, because tomorrow will surely be so hot again that it will be impossible to think or move.

It's strange that I so often run into children in the Metro during such late hours. Even today, a huge, mean-looking white woman came on at the very next station (her lips were surprisingly narrow and bloodless in contrast to her fleshy face), and a little black boy was hanging onto her. The woman settled in opposite me and with a short bark ordered the child to sit with her because he had absentmindedly wandered on. I wondered whether the child was adopted.

The little boy sat under the window beside me and, smiling shyly, started looking around. In his hands he held a plastic flowerpot in which a little flower was growing. Actually, on closer inspection, the flower hadn't been planted. It seemed to be the top of some bigger flower, like a daisy, that he had stuck into some gray soil. It seemed that they were coming from the country, or from the suburbs; they had bundles and bags. The boy placed the flowerpot on the window ledge and looked at it tenderly, he touched the soil, which was rather dry, from a park or flower bed, with his fingers. Clearly he intended to start growing this flower at home and had placed his hopes in this. The daisy was starting to droop quite visibly, because it had no roots.

I don't know what this thing called love is. Do you, Angelo? You're supposed to know everything. It's talked about so much, and it seems one should be chasing it in order not to waste one's life.

Did I love that person whose letters I went to look for in the mailbox, past the maple trees, underneath that sky, those letters that never arrived?

Once he himself arrived with the evening's express bus, that apparition of the Great World whose passing I had witnessed every evening, but this time it didn't whiz by but stopped obediently at the end of the grass-covered path that led to the pastorate, even though it was not a scheduled stop. He knew how to sweet-talk everyone, even drivers of express buses.

What did we do during this much-longed-for visit? We walked in the woods. It was October, cool and dusky. I'd secretly look at his face from the side. It was a very ordinary face, a little bit ragged, filling out already, just entirely typical of those parts. We didn't really have anything to talk about. Finally it started snowing, fine powdery snow, on the dormant grass, on the spruce trees, on our hair. I pretended that my hand accidentally touched his. His skin felt cold and lifeless. I could just as well have touched the bark of a spruce tree. I didn't write him anymore after that visit. And I just left the pastorate. Suddenly it was no more than he was, a discarded old house where the dead slammed doors and argued about their shares of the inheritance, about everything that had long since turned to dust.

And my adored correspondent? All that fascinating emptiness in which I had discovered him (on that bright spring day, in the grave-cold church) had disappeared. That grave was truly empty now, but empty without any kind of fascination, just as the churches here, empty old houses that people from all over the world traipse through for some reason. His fussing over youths who were studying to be confirmed, his blessing of flags, everything seemed hilarious to me. Suddenly he reminded me of an old woman who was airing all sorts of old rags that ought to have been burned much earlier. I didn't understand how he hadn't noticed that the century in which we met had been discarded as trash long ago, discarded along with everything else. He whose hands' power of enchantment I so admired at one time, how was it that he hadn't noticed that he ought to flee, even if it meant he would be naked and bloodied?

At least I escaped from there, from the place where I had to carry water up the stairs in pails and where, in the spring, the earth behind the window smelled as if at any moment it had a great secret message to declare. I exchanged the apartment Grandmother had left me for the one from which I watched the trams pass. Behind the tram stop was a half-finished building. Concrete columns and two big cranes stood in the open sky, always in the same position, because historical events had occurred in the interim and many building projects had been stopped.

Franz once enthusiastically told me that I came from a country where history was being made on a daily basis. He claimed to envy me because nothing much was supposed to happen here, in these still waters, anymore. They've talked about a crisis for five years, but no one is supposed to know what that means or where this crisis is supposed to come from.

"At least in your country something real is happening," Franz used to sigh.

I assured him that one can do very well without reality and history being made. It's even a lot more comfortable. But for him not to worry, for the day will probably come when the cranes will stop here, too. Why build houses, after all?

So I sat in that postwar building, in the high-ceilinged apartment, and looked through those dingy windows (you can wash them as much as you like, windows there are always dirty) at trams stopping, and the sun, which in the winter set at exactly the same spot between the immobile cranes and the concrete columns at around three o'clock. I could witness this historical panorama only when G. was not at home, because when he was home, then we either fought or went to bed. He is five years younger than I, and he stubbornly claimed to love me. Whenever anyone tells me that, it makes me want to run away, because the person who says that invariably has an expression that demands at least three drops of blood, if not your life, in return.

I constantly kept telling him that I did not love him and not to talk about it. But he was stubborn. He had taken it into his head and he just kept repeating, "I cannot live without you."

On the other hand, physical closeness binds one in a certain way, regardless of words or anything else, and with this G. I didn't feel myself so alone. Besides, I had my translations, which were going quite well and which helped pass the time and made me worry less about everything. I even felt strong enough to want to be totally alone, to wake up singing in the mornings and to start working, to go out occasionally, to visit people, to imagine some impossible love . . .

Actually, at that time I was secretly in love with someone else. I had seen him only once, socially, and had only exchanged a few words with him. I'd heard he'd gone to live in Sweden, so there was no danger of my running into him. I kept seeing him in my dreams.

I told G. to leave, but he wouldn't, kept insisting that he loved me and couldn't live without me, etc. Then I bought a puppy so that he could take it for walks, to get me off his mind. But he always left the puppy in my care. Once, when I was gone, he even took it to his mother's place. She naturally hated me, so she came and, figuratively speaking, threw the puppy in my face. In reality she couldn't do that because the dog was quite big by then, with drooping ears and sturdy paws. It was called Bear. Nor could the mother hit me, even though she may have wanted to, because then the dog would have bitten her. It loved me. With dogs it's even worse than with humans. You can tell them whatever you want to and they still look at you with that terribly faithful expression.

In the end it was G. who hit me, and I hit him back because I thought he would kill me. That very day Bear jumped on a spike, which pierced his chest, and I had to spend the day running around to vets getting him shots. In the evening at the tram stop I saw the person I had often seen in my dreams. He was there with his wife and infant daughter. His wife was young and beautiful, and they seemed very happy.

Do you recall the Sunday evening when we visited your friend Jean-Pierre? That was exactly two months ago today. So it's been exactly two months since we met, because it was that Sunday. You asked whether I'd like to go with you to a friend's, because you had to go there. If I had time and wouldn't mind, we could have a cup of tea at Jean-Pierre's . . . Well, you know I always have time and no objections.

This Jean-Pierre is the strangest person I have met in this phantasmal city, at the end of this century. I always recall his Barbie dolls as I move among people on the streets, in the museums, in the Metro . . . They were so quiet on those shelves, wearing clothes Jean-Pierre himself had sewed. Some were naked, painted gold or silver.

Remember, he told us he was working on a composition entitled *Barbie in Prison as Joan of Arc* just then. The prison was already finished, glued together. And you asked, "But the horse?" Of course there was no horse, because who would put a horse in prison? Joan went to prison without a horse.

He was very businesslike, this Pierrot. He served us strawberries with yogurt and explained that there was no point in buying fruit from street vendors even if it costs less. So many people may have touched it that it would probably spoil faster. The difference in price is illusory.

His Barbie dolls, on the other hand, were extraordinarily realistic. He had photographed them in various poses: Barbie's birthday (I wonder how old she was; I didn't think to ask); a burglar has intruded into Barbie's apartment and wounded her with a knife, blood everywhere; Barbie's burglar being guillotined; a whole series of photos of Barbie's funeral; Barbie in a casket amid roses, the mourners, the tomb . . .

Jean-Pierre explained that he had submitted his photos to Barbie magazines but they wouldn't be published because they did not meet the standards for the ads. We looked at one such magazine, published in the United States. There was a story there about a terrible crime. A thief had broken into the house of a famous millionaire Barbie collector and had set the house on fire on leaving, to destroy clues (he had no interest in the Barbie collection, only money and valuables). There were about ten thousand victims, some rare and very valuable.

I also remember that Jean-Pierre played a CD of nature sounds: bird songs, cuckoos calling, distant cowbells, the babbling of a brook.

I recalled this visit to tell you about the dream I had today. I saw in my dream that I was a Barbie doll and that the French police stopped me on the street and asked for my passport. I showed them my Soviet passport, which is outdated. The police told me it was only valid in public toilets and ordered me to undress. I took off my clothes and didn't mind. I felt very vindicated to have tricked the police because beneath the clothes was this cool, chaste doll's body made of plastic.

Today I lay underneath a linden tree in the park and stared at the sky. There was a bed of roses nearby. Roses fall apart so fast in this heat. I listened to petals dropping one by one, without a break. Maybe all this happened in the sky. There was a cloud . . .

It seems that I have very little to tell you. I almost don't want to talk anymore, even with you, unforgettable Angelo. This testimony of my life as a human person is coming to an end. My voice has become so weak that the girl in the bakery can hardly hear me. I have to point to the bread with my finger. Pretty soon she won't see me, either. I won't be able to go there anymore. Grass doesn't grow in bakeries. Grass grows elsewhere, by itself.

Living alone in Franz's apartment, I awoke every morning to the sound of the garbage truck. Cars were continually passing on the narrow street next to the river, and occasionally some would stop in front of the house. Yet it was always the garbage truck that awoke me around seven in the morning. The sun would already be up, and a bird would be singing in a tree by the river.

It seemed then as if the city had suddenly fallen silent; only the garbage truck droned in front of the house. I listened with my heart pounding as the garbage collectors dragged garbage bins across the yard. They're on plastic wheels. Then the truck started to whine angrily, and a bitter diesel smell entered the room through the open window. These trucks have built-in compactors for compressing garbage. I've seen it. After whining for a short time, it drove off. Only after several moments did the sounds of the city reemerge, the endless flow of cars on the opposite shore. An ambulance or fire truck honked incessantly somewhere when it was caught in traffic. A big fat bird (Uncle Ernst would call it a wild dove) calling from amid the sounds of the forest in the middle of a long bright day can call and call, without ever being able to escape from that forest or from that great prison of summer.

Sometimes I dozed off again, but as a rule I didn't fall asleep anymore after the garbage truck. I'd get up and start the coffee machine. I threw the previous day's coffee along with the filter into a garbage bag, which would rustle quietly. It would be a Franprix or Monoprix plastic shopping bag, or some other blue or pink plastic bag, in which I'd brought home fruit from the Arab. Franz had told me he never purchased garbage bags (you know, the black ones). He too was slightly Green, favoring ecological awareness.

While the coffee was dripping into the carafe, I'd sit by the window and light the day's first cigarette. Sometimes I wouldn't draw more than a single puff. I'd look into the tiny little yard, which only kitchen windows seemed to look out on. Anyway, the shutters were always closed. The garbage bin down in the shade, which the sun didn't reach even during midday, was bright green, empty again, and expectant. Later

I'd tie the garbage bag into a knot, sealing all evidence of my life within it—yogurt containers, plastic mineral-water bottles, grapefruit peels, cheese containers, deodorant sticks that I'd tired of. Then, carrying this featherweight little bundle in my hand, I'd creep into the yard and drop it into the bin. Sometimes it would still be totally empty, and when I lifted the lid, a faint sour smell would rise. Yesterday's garbage. The powerless stench of death, of erased life.

The following morning I'd be on the alert again, on the lookout for the garbage truck. The garbage collectors had to come through the front door and pass by the landing in order to reach the bins. The front door closed. Steps echoed. I waited. Were they coming up? What if they had orders to take the residents along as well? In brief, humans aren't necessary for garbage production anymore. Machines work just as well. Display items on shop counters doze in the alluring glare of artificial light, dreaming of garbage bins. Automatic teller machines hum silently. Money is circulating. Lights in offices turn off during lunch hours. There is nothing to remind us of humans anymore, just as there is nothing to remind us of yesterday's garbage.

I'm sitting and glowering at the telephone. The telephone is a small white thing on the wall, with an innocently drooping cord. It looks as though it's totally unaware of what is going on. It doesn't deceive me, of course, but neither can I catch it red-handed. I glower at it for hours, until it becomes a white dot in the empty distance. Your voice, Angelo, should come from somewhere out there to inform me of the court's decision. I don't want to be caught sleeping. That's why I'm on my guard.

Behind me there's an open window, and when the telephone has just about dissolved in my vision and the voice seems to have started on its way, I suddenly hear the fluttering of wings behind me, the sounds of running and laughter, which rattle the treetop like hail. I start and turn around. Outside the day is bright behind the window. Nothing out of the ordinary is to be seen on the ground or in the sky. That's when it rings.

Just as it rang that time in the apartment on Île Saint-Louis. When everything was over. When silence ensued. Only Mozart's symphony, the *Adagio* by now, continued to be exuded from the compact disc, packing the silence in its translucent plastic. It had happened so fast. Suddenly he had been caught in the grip of his pain. Suddenly he noticed nothing beyond it. Suddenly he had collapsed around the last reality of his world. And then he had let go even of that. I was alone in the apartment, alone with the silence. The plastic was suffocating me. Mozart's symphony didn't let me breathe. I had the feeling that I was paper-thin and hollow inside, that I would soon dissolve into the pale evening outside the window, into the emptiness hovering above the river.

That's when the telephone rang. That ringing restored some feeling of weight. I felt my flesh once more, my heart, which had started to beat wildly, the sweat that was dripping down my back.

The telephone rang a couple of times and then started talking. The automatic answering machine was on. The voice talked cheerily and confidently, but I couldn't understand a word. I only felt the constantly increasing pressure of my body on the floor. Then came a quiet click and a few short signals. Everything was quiet once more. I had the irresistible urge to listen to that chipper voice again, and again. It came from the world of the living and it had restored my flesh. I would have wanted to crawl into that voice, just like an oyster into its shell.

I crept to the telephone, pressed the message button, and listened to the voice on the machine, the voice that had been human a few moments earlier, which asked calmly and confidently that it be called back at number such and such. Asked that he call back, he who had just let go of his pain. I listened to that pleasant, carefree voice many times, demanding the impossible without a moment's hesitation. In the end this calmed me. That which had happened a few moments earlier had happened years earlier. I emptied both glasses into the sink, let the water run a little. Then dropped the glasses into the garbage bag, tied it in a knot, took it in my hand, and rapidly walked out the door, out of the house, on the street, far away.

I don't know how far I walked. Anyway, it seems it was far enough because they haven't caught me. Nor will they. I'm sitting here in my room. The telephone is ringing. I grasp the receiver, but it's not you, Angelo. It's the wrong number. He asks for someone whose name I've never heard, who may have lived here before me.

Sometime, when I've left this place (I'd like to be going already even though I haven't received my certificate yet, but so what, so what if I don't finish?), they may call and ask for me, and someone may answer that he has never heard such a name. Or the telephone may ring in an empty room. The world is full of telephones that ring in empty rooms and automatic answering machines that repeat words meant for the dead.

You know, yesterday I bought a mango from the Arab and ate it. I had looked at those fruits on his counter for a long time but had never dared to buy one because I'd never tasted a mango before. Inside, close to the pit, it smells a little like resin, like spruce trees on very warm days when they melt like candles in the sun. Otherwise they're bright yellow and sweet. That mango reminded me that I should continue to follow the sun, that I haven't arrived yet. I realized that today as I left the house and crossed the white graveled square, which shimmered from heat. I went as always, head bent, sweat dripping from my forehead, resigned to the hot air.

The sun here is hot but not harsh enough. There's still a softness in the heat that penetrates the smog and torches roses and the metal on cars.

This mango came from the Ivory Coast.

In short, I should go to Lisbon. There's a poem by Pessoa that says "sunshine is, only in Lisbon"; I think about it constantly. I should go to Lisbon to check it out.

Have you read Pessoa? I know that if I asked you this on the telephone, you would answer that you were totally ignorant, that you haven't read a book in your life. Who knows? Maybe you really haven't. Maybe it's not just a boast. That would be something!

I, for example, am a victim of books. I've written some poetry, bad, of course. Everyone there wrote poetry. It was a national hobby, like soccer in England. They also read it, and poems were ascribed much more significance than they actually had. That was another mistake of Eastern Europe in the nineteenth century.

Pessoa has two more verses like that:

> Deserts are vast, and all is desert,
> mistakes excepted, of course.

You're right, Angelo, one is forced to deceive more and more every day. Once you've started on the road of deception, there's no turning back; the deceit has to grow so that people believe it, so they won't dare call it deception, that would be "too horrible."

I love deceivers, clear-eyed deceivers, like you, Angelo. Sweet scoundrels who deceive knowingly. I'd like to be accepted as one of them.

I especially liked what you told me about your work. Is it really true that as a coffee expert you know absolutely nothing about coffee? That you just charmed those directors with your arrogant gaze? That you just sip from the cup they give you, smack your lips, put on a thoughtful mien and after a meaningful pause let drop from your deceptive lips,

"Lemon."

Or "Sour vanilla."

Or "Rancid."

And sales directors of firms revise their documents, change agreements; faxes whirl angrily, ships set out; in Africa or Latin America one poor community is hit by famine, the other by an economic boom.

And you, my angelic, insolent friend, are introduced to new sales directors as the "eminent botanist."

Franz should have been a little more blatantly deceptive; that would surely have saved him. I couldn't tolerate the way he always accentuated the positive.

For example, he owned stocks, which he had inherited from his parents. I discovered this accidentally when I caught him poring over stock prices in the business section of the newspaper, his nape bent like a monk's at prayer. I asked what he was studying and he, somewhat embarrassed, answered, prices of his stocks.

"But anyway, they're going down," he added quickly, as if to offer an excuse. It turned out that his family owned a "certain" part of some business that made warplanes, among other things.

"But the civilian production is increasing constantly, hopefully especially now, in the new world order when there's less of a demand for warplanes," he assured me. Owning these stocks apparently didn't agree with his otherwise leftist leanings, but in the end he claimed that it didn't really matter who owned the stocks, that it would not make any difference.

I was surprised that he would try to justify himself and asked whether he didn't find warplanes beautiful. Didn't he enjoy imagining how everything would be bombed to smithereens with his planes one day?

He made a face at this kind of talk, as if I had shown him something disgusting, and told me I was talking nonsense.

I tried to turn it into a joke, but I understood that I had crossed a boundary and that there were things one didn't discuss even jokingly. He had insisted that everything was not a joke.

I wonder what everything is then, if it's not a joke. I wonder what it meant when I read Franz's name with the word "suicide" in the newspaper. It stated this as a fact. Like a juicy fact, by the way, because a prominent politician had just committed suicide, and everything that smelled of suicide was a tidbit for the papers. That's probably why no one became suspicious. Everything was so routine.

■ □ ■ □ ■

Let's not talk about that trip anymore, my poor
darling, it seems we haven't done anything else for a
long time, and now it's becoming tiring. Like long
yawns that exhaust pain, overlong expectations deplete
all happiness.

Madame de Sévigné to her daughter,
Monday, July 11, 1672

YES, HOPING IS LIKE AN ILLNESS. IT SEEMS TO ME THAT I HAVE
finally improved, that I no longer hope, that I'm ready to
feel pain again.

The heat has passed for now. I went for a walk in the park
this evening. What coolness! I was wearing only a light silk
shirt and sensed this blessing with my entire body. Just like
back in the North during summer evenings when you're
coming home somewhere along a rural road. You've stayed
too late. The sun has dropped beyond the woods. It's close to
midnight, and you can feel the damp coolness of the meadow
through your cotton shirt.

Today was the Feast of Corpus Christi. I watched a procession at the nearby monastery, a pathetically small crowd with
pictures and church banners. An old man carried a wooden
figure of Christ on the cross. It was obviously too heavy for
him. The crucifix was very realistic. The wounds and blood

looked genuine and made me want to cover them with plantain leaves, to make the fever finally pass.

There were very few people in the park today compared to those stifling evenings when the air would barely move across the pond, only some stray souls. Today was too cold for taking walks! The few who were there were probably my coconspirators, my kindred. It's quite probable that they also paused by the cedars of Lebanon, where it smells of resin, or let the shadows of the beech tree caress their limbs, or pressed their vanishing faces into the blossoms of the late-flowering jasmine, in hopes of finding sweet sedation.

A man was sitting on the bench, straight as a tulip, reading a book.

My dear Angelo, isn't it true that plants yearn for the sun, even though unrelenting sun makes their blossoms wither and urges seeds toward ripening and death? On the other hand, rain and coolness give them relief, let them stretch their stems, let them drowsily close their crowns and spread their leaves ever wider.

You can see that I haven't managed to go anywhere yet, and I have little left to write to you. But I don't know how to stop writing. I can't imagine what it will be like when I no longer talk to you. At some point, after all, one has to find an ending, once the beginning was found. Even if it takes force. The ending may involve force.

What do I do? I walk through my long, empty days where no one and nothing await me. I let myself be dragged up the escalator to the Beaubourg library, where I find a line. I don't intend to stand in line, because lines for me have the smell of moldy smoked sausage. Grandmother used to send me to stand in line for sausage, whenever the store sold it at the reduced state-fixed price. "Go get a place in line, I'll come in half an hour," she'd say. It was boring and stifling waiting in line. People in the back would push forward, hoping that by doing so they would ensure that some would still be left by the time their turn came. Later that smoked sausage would sit in the refrigerator forever. Grandmother cut only very thin slices. I was forced to eat it even though it was disgusting. It was like Holy Communion, only instead of bread, it was meat, tough and moldy on the sides. "One can still eat it," Grandmother said. "What's the harm in mold? We can wipe it off!"

So I ride down again with the escalator. People's heads are moving past me in the upward direction, not downward as before. I'm wearing a Walkman, listening to Handel, Bach, or U2; I'm deaf like that nineteenth-century woman in the film, and dumb besides. I'm afraid to look at my watch, afraid that it's still too early. To deceive the watch I go to the Louvre where heads again move past me, the stone heads of Greeks and Romans long dead.

One place to escape from time is in bookstores, small ones that don't have too many books. Actually, there are too many books even in these, but not depressingly too many as in the FNAC. In those smaller stores one can take some volume at random and read it, a book that somehow catches attention: by its title, or the author's strange name, which may be reminiscent of something, or the picture on the front cover . . . There is no literature anymore, there are just single books that arrive in bookstores, just as letters, newspapers, advertising pamphlets arrive in mailboxes. Someone tells his story in these, expresses his thoughts, invites others . . . It's totally irrelevant whether one reads or does not read these books.

World literature! That sounds just as hollow as "peace-keeping force." Some kind of world literature may still exist in the brain of some well-intentioned literature professor in Eastern Europe.

I particularly enjoy amateurish novels that have been published by some back-alley publishing house. Sometimes after reading entire chapters of them in those bookstores, I feel carefree for the rest of the day, as if some unhappy soul had held my hand and hesitatingly told me about all his suffering, and I had nodded understandingly: Yes, exactly, you know, it's just the same for me!

Books in bookstores are still new and clean, unread in any case. Strange flesh hasn't touched them yet. There they are light and random, not like in libraries, where they weigh on shelves and may at any moment fall through ceilings, thick and grease-stained reminders of those disgusting words:

Mandatory Literature!

Ignorant Bumpkin!

Our History!

I hate libraries! What would I look for there? Pretend to be some distinguished aristocrat? Deny the old Singer sewing machine strap, the *People's Voice,* and the bedbugs that crawled out from behind the wallpaper torn loose from the paneling to fatten themselves on my blood every night?

When I leave the bookstore it has started to rain. The wind is cold and mean, bending trees. As far as I know, this kind of weather is appropriate for June only in the country I came from. I have brought the weather along from home and have unwrapped it, just like the meat pastries that were brought along on trips. Food from home always had to be brought along whenever Grandmother and I visited her half brother and his wife in the country. That happened once or twice a year, and those were the only trips we ever took. Nor did I ever go anywhere by myself, only on class excursions in the spring.

I waited for those trips for months: "How many more days to Uncle Ernst's birthday?" I would pester Grandmother. If it had been up to me, we would have gone right away, without waiting another minute, by the first train, hands in our pockets. But Grandmother prepared thoroughly for leaving home. The day before, she would bake pastries filled with meat, to take as a present for her half brother ("Who would go empty-handed?") and also to eat on the trip. One absolutely had to take food for trips, although in my opinion we could just as well have bought meat-filled pastries from the diner at the station. Grandmother disdained those, but I yearned for them and swore to myself that when I grew up I'd always buy meat pastries from the diner at the station.

"Who knows whether they're edible," Grandmother doubted. No, food always had to be brought along. The trip could drag on, last for days and weeks, could end up God knows where! I guess Grandmother had her own experience with trains. She never took her kerchief off in the train or unbuttoned her coat, even though the compartment may have been warm. And she kept the bundle with the meat pastries and her medicines on her lap the entire trip. The train ride to the country took some three hours. The distance was barely a hundred kilometers, but the train was slow, with wooden seats (it was called the "wooden" train). It stopped at all the stations, sometimes in the middle of spruce forests, other times in the middle of birch forests, to let out mushroom hunters wearing jogging pants and carrying plastic pails. In the meantime I pestered Grandmother for meat pastries. I wasn't hungry, but just to pass the time. Eating was part of those trips to the country. As far as I can remember, the main activity there was eating, and talking about eating. Granduncle's wife had a cow, and she would give me fresh milk: "Drink heartily, you don't get this in town!"

"That city milk is nothing more than blue water, doesn't even stain the bottle," my grandmother agreed. I noticed that she praised everything there. We got our potatoes for the winter from Ernst.

Basically our diet was sauce and potatoes. Cow's milk made me nauseated and gave me diarrhea. I would poke at my plate and embarrass Grandmother. I was amazed by how much sauce and potatoes Ernst and his wife managed to eat. They would say, "Let's eat up and go pick potatoes. First let's bring the horse from the collective farm." That meant that I would go along with Ernst and later rattle on the wagon on the boring, dusty road among the alder brush. Mainly it was boring in the country and I would immediately start yearning for the city, for our apartment and my school, which wouldn't be in session yet.

I always yearned to go to the country, but there time passed even more slowly. Actually, all I had wanted was to get away. The days were even longer in the country than in the city. Thick grass and alder brush grew everywhere. One always had to look out not to step in cow dung. The only fun thing was sleeping, because I was made a bed from two easy chairs pushed together, and I pretended that it was a ship that would take me far away. Fast, so that the days and years would just flash by.

I could use such a ship even now. A ship that would take me through life at a faster pace, so that my watch wouldn't frighten me anymore.

Or a ship that would at least take me far from Ernst's potato patch, where I'm still standing today, my hands in my pants pockets, watching the wind rustle potato plants, without knowing what to do next.

Still here. It's raining. The leaves of the ash tree startle with a downward motion whenever a raindrop hits them: the keys of a mute piano. I bought a bottle of cheap wine from the store. Pour some into a plastic glass and stir in sugar, otherwise it's too sour. This slowly deadens the pain, hides it under a warm numbness that starts at the feet and creeps upward. There is no pain, by the way. I just made that up now, to amuse you, to sound more literary.

I hate writing essays. But I think I already mentioned that. I think I've really said all there is to say. What then should I do now? Wait? Life passes so slowly. If I could close my eyes, doze, in your nearness, your warmth, until it's over . . . What am I saying? I disdained the closeness and warmth I was offered, now I have to be content. What more do I want?

Do I want my face to be gilded, to be wrapped in fragrant creams and placed in a stone casket that no voice could penetrate? Like that Egyptian boy I saw today at the Louvre (one can go there because it doesn't rain on one's head). He had been removed from the casket, by the way, and had been put into a glass case for viewing. One can never be certain. Even graves are opened to let the world's inhabitants march through.

At the Louvre a mattress caught my eye. I had to touch it to be sure: marble. It seemed too soft, as though the stone statue were resting on real upholstery. The mattress was eighteenth-century work, the figure antique. Different centuries', different eras' idea of sleep, different conceptions of softness, all brought together. The name of the statue was *The Sleeping Hermaphrodite.* From the hall it looked exactly like a woman, but up close and examined from the other side it was a man. I observed the dilemma one couple was having.

"But it's intentionally made like that!" scolded the man.

"Do you think so?" doubted the woman.

I didn't want what I was supposed to have wanted. When Franz returned from Strasbourg and Geneva (it was another long weekend, Whitsunday I think, yes, Pentecost), he asked me what my plans were. My fellowship would soon be ending, but he could easily arrange for me to stay on, a kind of "extension" (he omitted to add that then I would be entirely beholden to him). I surely wouldn't want to return "there," would I?

I answered that I wasn't planning anything. Maybe I'd go back; how did I know? I must have looked rather listless and passive, because Franz became angry and started yelling at me. He grabbed me by the shoulders and shook me. As I was being shaken I thought resignedly, Do what you want with me. The day was hot. I was half asleep. He shouted, "You're crazy! No normal person would refuse what I'm willing to give you, but you want to go back there . . . there . . . there!" (He never did find the right word.)

That's when I suddenly woke up, when it became clear to me that I had to bring this to a close, that none of them would ever catch me and that I would never want what I was supposed to want. At the last moment I would always slip out of their hands!

I was no longer apathetic. I looked Franz in the eye and said, "No, of course I won't go back there." He didn't understand right away. I had to repeat what I had said. Then he smiled tenderly, hugged me almost like a brother, and asked to be forgiven.

"Forgive me. I lost my cool. But you know, I couldn't stand your expression, such total lack of willpower. It wasn't even . . . human!"

All of a sudden he was tender and calm, this Franz. Things were going the way they were supposed to. The world's order had slipped but now had been restored. I went into the kitchen to make gin and tonics.

Did I mention that he occasionally took some drops for his heart? Nothing serious, just to ease the fear of death. Once he'd told me, "It's a harmless tonic, homeopathic medicine actually, totally without any taste, by the way. But if I took just half of this bottle, I'd be dead."

The thought agitated him.

Because he then added, "I tried it once. They revived me. It made no sense."

I went to the refrigerator and opened the door. You already know what followed. Almost. I added the entire bottle of heart medicine into one glass of gin and tonic. The other had just gin and tonic.

This is the last letter I am going to write, Angelo. I'm not sure I even want to write you anymore. You seem distant, even a pointless fantasy. But still, I started this testimony once and I better finish it. Testimony? I've read bits and pieces of what I've written. Is there even a shred of truth in it?

The truth is rather that I found these letters on a computer disk, in the Seine. Yes, like in reeds where they used to find babies who had been left in baskets to flow downstream with the river. Like they find people who have drowned in this river even today.

It was late. The night was warm, almost suffocating. The huge city was having difficulty breathing and was turning from side to side in its sweaty bed. I wandered over bridges and along quays. Finally, like a sleepwalker, I descended to the lowest quay by the water's edge at the end of Île Saint-Louis, by the Sully-Morland Square. That's where the river suddenly turns wide and wild, where it's dark because the city lights don't reach that far. In the distance a Metro train crossed the bridge, like a phantom. It came from the underground after all.

I stood by the water's edge, not really thinking anything, barely noticing the coolness rising from the river. Whispers sounded in the park. Someone disappeared into the bushes. Someone moaned, either from pain or from pleasure. Someone whistled piercingly on the bridge. I was in a daze from the heat and the emptiness of a day that had been too long, from the sensuous night wallowing around me. I was staring dully at the oil slick glowing in the water when suddenly I saw a hand, a white, seemingly dry hand extending something toward me. I didn't have time to think. I reached for the hand. I wanted to grab *the hand,* to pull, or to be pulled. I don't know which. It seemed a command as well as an invitation. I reached toward the water, almost lost my balance, grabbed the hand, but found only this slim package in my fist.

The hand was gone. Another Metro train was crossing the bridge, in the opposite direction. A gust of wind rippled the water and suddenly sobered me, though I'd only had one bottle of beer. I don't remember what time it was by then . . .

My Writer, I have tried to find you in this town, have chased after you along platforms in the Metro. But on the escalators when you have looked back, your face has been that of an indifferent stranger. I have sat in cafés and tried to penetrate beyond the sunglasses, but some gesture by the object of my observation has always revealed my mistake:

it has not been you. I don't even know your name, and that's why in my thoughts I started calling you by the name of your—and my—beloved correspondent. You did call him your mirror and your double, didn't you? Besides, angels can be of either gender. Unfortunately, they show themselves to us very rarely. And even then our awareness of their presence is always only after the fact. He was here, something changed, nothing is the same anymore. But there is no way for me to get back to that moment, and if there were, would I even recognize myself there anymore?

How many times have I gone back to that quay by the water's edge, the spot where the river suddenly becomes wide and wild, and where in the distance the Metro trains cross the bridge, riding through darkness as though through water, as if the world were submerged in water, on the other side, not here where we belong? I look at the surface of the water as if it were a boundary behind which the real world begins. I wait for your hand to extend from the water, at least for circles to form on the surface, as a sign that I have permission to come. But nothing happens. Only a breeze ripples the water and makes the tall trees rustle above my head. Someone's moans, whether from pain or from pleasure, mingle with the rustling. Someone's piercing whistle sounds from the bridge even though not a soul is there. Someone's passion is being satisfied. Someone falls dead on grass that was just moistened by the seed of another. The flesh all around me is willing, Angelo, but there is no spirit anywhere.

It just remains for me to forward this final letter to you. I don't want to keep anything to myself now that you know everything anyway.

The letter is the following:

A long time has passed in the interim, a week or even more. Anyway, many letters and notices had accumulated in my mailbox. I sat on the bed and read them in about ten minutes. This seemed to exhaust the time I had been absent. Nothing, ten minutes.

And yet it was I who walked beneath the stars, along the road between the villages, lost, and the wind carried with it the smell of sea and of hay. Exactly, the smell of sea and hay. That certainly was not imagined. But perhaps I remember even that from some other place, from there, from the lost century? Just as the village store where I sat beside the empty crates on the steps, next to the empty highway, underneath a warning light which lit up my unfamiliar hands?

No, in any case it could not have been there, because there you don't see stars in June. Nights are too light. And there, there are no highways.

Yes, once I stood by the side of an expressway, a four-lane highway. You're not allowed to stand there. Humans have no place there. Even cars are allowed to stop only if the driver senses his death nearing. I was standing on the edge of the highway. The sun was scorching my already burned face and cars were whizzing by. I couldn't be bothered lifting my hand to stop them. I thought they couldn't see me, because the sunlight was too bright.

There was a field next to the highway, full of poppies, and a woman was pulling grass by the edge of the field. Her gray skirt had been rolled up. That may have been a thousand years ago. The field was billowing and glimmering. She put the bundle of grass down, straightened herself up, and raised her hand as a sunshade, to look at something. What? Cars on the highway, which were dashing into the shimmering sun like insects into the fire? Could she see them? Or to look at me? I was standing on the boundary. I could not be seen by either the flying phantoms who were melting in their own speed or that woman who was gathering grass for her animals' evening fodder. The day was already drawing to evening. The woman had sturdy brown legs, and the poppies touched the edge of her rolled-up skirt.

I once saw the words "border state" in a newspaper. That was how they labeled the country from which I came. It was a political term. Very appropriate, by the way. A border state is nonexistent. There is something on one side and something on the other side of the border, but there is no border. There is a highway, and a field of grain with a farmhouse under tall, thirsty trees, but where is the border between them? It's invisible. And if you should happen to stand on the border, then you too are invisible, from either side.

I never got to Lisbon, by the way. The car that picked me up near Paris turned into a side road, drove in the other direction, and I went along, west, in any case toward the sea.

That's where something strange happened to me, as if I had been ill before but now became well. Where? Was it in that village hotel where the church bells started pealing right next to my ear the moment I opened the window, on the other side of a totally empty square? No, not there, not yet. That was probably where I started on the actual road to recovery, loosened the reins, hoisted the load onto my back and discovered that it was so light.

Along with the villagers I even went to the mass those bells had announced. It was nothing significant or important, just a small step on the road that I had started, content and resigned all of a sudden, ready for anything. Really, nothing special. A few light blue and pink Virgins, a priest who spoke with a habitual sweetness, and some weird wooden jaws, which glowered beneath the ceiling. The song they sang there admonished people to not be afraid and to "dance on the heels of God." The priest was the same man who had accosted me in that old church in Amsterdam, the same blue-eyed beggar for whom I had fried potatoes and cut pickles in my dream.

I sat at the back, apart from the villagers. A man, neither old nor young, around forty, sat in my pew. He held his hands in his pocket and his mouth tightly closed. Only when they memorialized the dead did he seem to liven up. He was probably there because of someone who had died, either his wife or his mother. Most likely his mother because he was that kind of rural man, large and robust, someone who may have lived with his mother and now had no one to talk with, least of all with God.

That was on Saturday evening. Afterward I walked along a small road that led from the church to the sea. Roses, heavy with flowers slightly drooping from the day's heat, with leaves already perking up in the evening's coolness, were leaning against white garden walls. Then came a field of dense, thick wheat; rows of flowering potatoes, already in shadows cast by pine trees; voracious cows on a hillside.

Then, one morning I was on my way toward the lighthouse. It was on an island far in the sea, beyond which one couldn't go. And the lighthouse in turn was at the tip of the island. Beyond it were only wild cliffs and breakers, the site of shipwrecks.

The sun woke me in my hotel room at six o'clock, as soon as it had risen on a naked world. The hotel was an old building, the last one, high above the harbor where boats at low tide ended up on mud, as though they never intended to move again. The clothes closet in my room had three doors. The center door was a mirror. In the evening I had studied myself in this mirror and then crept out on the stairs. Everyone in the house was already asleep. At regular intervals a strange light kept flashing in the window of the stairwell. At first I didn't realize what it was, but after reaching to look, I saw it was the beam from the lighthouse, twirling in proud circles through the air.

The morning sunlight immediately brightened the window, and I was glad to have the chance to visit the lighthouse. It was still cool outside, thick dew on the ground everywhere. The hotel steward was putting umbrellas up on the patio. A woman in her tiny garden was already bending over hydrangeas and rhubarbs. That was at about the last house, with white and blue shutters, next to a vast empty expanse. As I passed her she straightened up. It was the same woman who had said "Little dog" in the Metro, the same woman I had seen beside the highway picking grass from the field. I greeted her, because it seemed strange to pass without speaking, and she greeted me back and smiled kindly, kindly and indifferently, and then she bent over her flowers again.

One of the windows was open, and I caught a glimmer of the drowsy secret that rooms hold in mornings. A cat was sitting on a windowsill, licking herself. The lighthouse was still a long way away but already visible in its entirety.

Actually, there wasn't very much at the lighthouse. Low gray grass, with yellow flowers, bending with the wind. Enormous red-colored rocks. Some sheep.

Maybe there was something else. I don't exactly know. Anyway, I can't tell you more, not even you, dear Angelo. It's my secret.

Now I'm back in the city, since the day before yesterday, or whenever it was. Five hundred kilometers on the expressway in an open car is as good as four hours in the same spot in the desert. There were traffic jams outside Paris. I didn't realize before how small this city with its pleasant cafés and boulevards actually is, just a little tourist village. The real city is out there where the corrugated steel and concrete reinforcements are heated by an insolent sun. Commercial centers to which heavy trucks haul new goods. Traffic jams where people die every day, in heat and exhaust fumes, on their way to vacations or homes or department stores. The garbage dump lies waiting at the very end.

I'm out of money. In a small town near the sea, where I had ended up, an automatic teller machine swallowed my card. The street was totally empty. It was noon. The sun was shining and the shutter of the automatic teller window silently slid shut. I thought to myself, It's finished.

■ □ ■ □ ■

The wheat on the fields of Esquibien is not yet ripe,
My hunger is not yet ripe,
It has time to ripen.

The road curves through fertile fields
Toward the sea, toward the dunes,
Where grass scents the evening.

How can it be so sweet, O Lord?
And what flowers are these,
What fragrance?

Must I go to the shore at low tide
And gather fresh seashells?
Must I lift the heavy basket to my shoulders
And carry it to the threshold,
But what threshold?

Must I walk, eyes downcast,
Until the secret is revealed?

■ □ ■ □ ■

WRITINGS FROM AN UNBOUND EUROPE